A JOURNEY OF TERROR
FOR FREEDOM

"A sensitively written story, laced with touches of humor." —*The National Observer*

"Exciting and realistic." —*Columbus Dispatch*

"An excellent story and a very moving one." —*San Francisco Examiner Chronicle*

JANE KRISTOF was born in Chicago, Illinois. She is a graduate of the University of Chicago. For several years she taught at the Chicago City Junior Colleges, and also worked in remedial reading programs with disadvantaged youngsters. She holds a Ph.D. in Art History from Columbia University. Mrs. Kristof now lives in Palo Alto, California with her husband and son.

W. T. MARS was born in Poland and attended the Academy of Fine Arts in Warsaw. His art work has been exhibited in several countries, and he has illustrated numerous books. Now an American citizen, Mr. Mars lives on Long Island with his wife, Helene.

Steal Away Home

Jane Kristof

Illustrated by W. T. Mars

CAMELOT BOOKS/PUBLISHED BY AVON

AVON BOOKS
A division of
The Hearst Corporation
959 Eighth Avenue
New York, New York 10019

First Camelot Printing, December, 1970
Third Printing, December, 1971

CAMELOT TRADEMARK REG. U.S. PAT. OFF. AND
FOREIGN COUNTRIES, REGISTERED TRADEMARK—
MARCA REGISTRADA, HECHO EN CHICAGO, U.S.A.

Printed in the U.S.A

To my parents,
Donald S. and Mary McWilliams,
with affection and gratitude

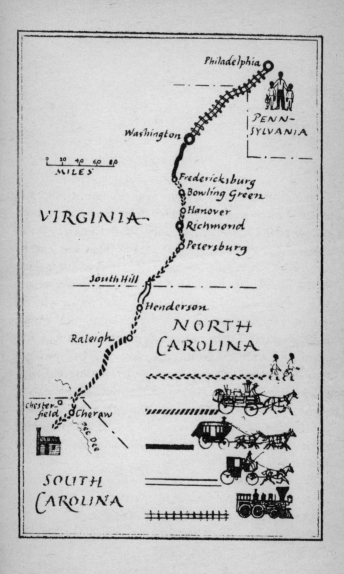

I WILL BEGIN the story of our escape where it begins in my own mind—in the little slave cabin where I was born and raised in Chesterfield County, South Carolina. It was a warm Sunday evening in May, 1853. That was a while back, and I've grown a lot and learned some since then, but I still remember that evening just as if it was yesterday: the warm air, the smell of smoke and cooking inside and honeysuckle outside, the nice feeling of Mama moving around in the cabin. My brother Obadiah was sitting alongside me in the doorway. We had just got back from a revival meeting and were eating our supper of thin soup and hoecake in the light of the setting sun. Mama hadn't gone to the meeting because our little sister was sick—she was sick almost all the time—so she was questioning us to see how concentrated we'd been.

"What was the hymns, Amos?" she started.

I remembered three or four for her.

"And Obie, what was the Preacher's text?"

Obie had been fidgeting most of the way through the

preaching and I didn't expect he'd know, so I tried to help him out.

"It was something about Abel, and then Noah, and then Abraham, and how they all had a lot of faith," I mumbled.

But Obie surprised me. He must have been listening after all because he remembered the Preacher's exact words, almost.

"Abraham, he was called to go out, and he went out not knowing whither . . ."

He turned and grinned at Mama, and looking into the gloom of the cabin I saw her long, dark face light up a little bit with pride.

"And, Mama, you know what? Preacher Prentice walked back over this way after the meeting and was visiting some and——" Obie stopped short and we both got to our feet as the Preacher himself, white haired and stooping, came round the corner of our cabin.

Preacher Prentice was just about everything we could hope to become. He was a freedman, he could read and write, and he worked for himself, traveling about the country with a horse and cart fixing and selling pots and pans. The white folks called him a tinker, but to us he was the Preacher.

"Saw you boys at the meeting, didn't I?" he asked.

We both nodded. We hoped he hadn't come to talk to Mama about Obie's behavior.

"Do I know your pa?"

I shook my head. "No, sir." And Obie explained, "Pa's been gone these five years. He belonged to Master Smithers, and they moved up to Maryland when we was little."

Mama joined us in the doorway now, and the Preacher looked at her, kind of screwing up his eyes.

"So you must be the wife of Henry that used to be hired out to do carpentry work."

"That's right," said Mama. "I'm Henry's wife. The Smithers moved away just after my little girl was born, and they took Henry along like the boy said."

"I used to know him a little," said the Preacher. Then he looked quickly around and lowered his voice. "Can I come inside a minute?"

Mama looked surprised, but she stepped back into the cabin. We all followed her. Then, standing away from the door, the Preacher started to fumble with the band around the inside of his hat and pulled out a much folded piece of paper. He handed it to Mama.

"I got a letter for you from Henry," he said. "I'd just been trying to find the right cabin without too much questioning. Here it is."

Mama studied the wrinkled piece of paper for a while. There was no excitement on her face, but I could see that the hand that held the letter was trembling. Then she handed it back to the Preacher.

"I can't read," she said softly.

The Preacher stood right beside the door, trying to get some of the failing light without letting himself be seen from the outside. It was hard for him to make out the words, and he read kind of haltingly.

"My dear wife, I am sorry that I did not write you for so long, but I could not send any more letters in the usual way."

"I reckon he don't want to send no more letters by Master Bricker," said Obie excitedly.

"Quiet, son," Mama said sharply, and the Preacher put a finger to his lips.

The letter went on: "Master Smithers took sick and died last October. He set me free in his will, so I went north. I have taken the name of Carpenter and am living in a small town called Lemhorn near the city of Philadelphia. There is a lot of building going on here and I always have work. I save everything I can, and I hope in maybe four years or even a little less I will have enough to make an offer to Master Bricker for you and little Sally. I wish Amos and Obadiah were here to help me. God bless and keep you all. Your loving husband."

For a minute nobody spoke. Then Mama said softly, "Four years." I couldn't tell whether she was sad or happy.

"What about us?" said Obie. "He says he's going to ask for Mama and Sally, but what about us?"

He sounded just about ready to cry, so I said quickly, "He said he wished we was there, Obie. But he don't have money, not for all four of us. He wants Mama the most, and Master would maybe sell Sally cheap 'cause she's sickly."

Obie cheered up a bit. "Maybe he wants us to run off and go north and help him."

Mama and I started to hush him up when the Preacher said slowly, "Maybe that's just what he do want."

We all stared at him. Obie was the most surprised of all at the idea that he might be right.

The Preacher went on. "He couldn't say just what he meant. He knows we got no privacy here, and even my letters get read at the post office before I ever see them. But that what he says about wishing Amos and Obadiah could be with him, that's written larger and darker than the rest of the letter. It's got to have some special meaning."

"But they're just little children," whispered Mama. "Amos, he's only twelve yet, and Obie's nine. And they're both small and skinny for their years."

The Preacher looked at us and rubbed his head. "I reckon they know how to do a full day's work though," he said.

We nodded. We'd had to know how. Every able-bodied slave worked from sunup to late afternoon on the Bricker plantation.

"And they don't look backward," the Preacher went on.

"No, indeed they ain't," said Mama. "They take after their pa. Amos, he's—well, he's careful beyond his years. He's been the man around here these five years, since he was just knee high. And my Obie," she smiled a little bit, "he could talk his way out of anything."

Obie was just bursting with excitement. "We could do it, Mama," he told her. "Me and Amos are real good walkers. Remember last Christmas we walked all the way to Searsville and back, and we weren't even tired. That must have been twelve miles at least. We could do it."

"We could try, Mama," I added, trying to sound braver than I felt.

Mama shook her head. "It must be hundreds and hundreds of miles. I don't know how far. . . . And they wouldn't even know the way."

That was true enough. We all knew that we lived in South Carolina and that North Carolina began just a little way past Searsville. But where was Philadelphia? We only knew that it was up north and very far away.

That didn't seem to worry the Preacher though. "There's folks that would help them along the way," he said. "I could put them on the underground railroad."

"The what?"

"The underground railroad." The Preacher explained that name which then meant nothing to us but soon would mean so much. The "railroad" was people, people who hid and helped runaway slaves and sent them on to the next "station" on the road north to freedom.

Mama was still shaking her head and saying how little we were when he finished explaining, but somehow I already knew we would go.

"You don't need to make up your mind right now," the Preacher said finally. "But if you decide, here's what you can do. Do Master Bricker give you a day off July 4th?"

We nodded.

"Well, the Fourth comes on a Monday this year. If you was to slip away Saturday night or Sunday morning early, you'd have two days' start before anyone would notice you was gone. You should be able to walk to the new bridge over the Pee Dee River in that time. It's no more than twenty-five miles, I reckon. Well, you sit there on the river bank under the bridge—no one can see you—and I'll be along with my cart sometime on July 5th. I'll stop near the bridge and go down to the river for some water. When I start singing that means it's safe for you to come out from under the bridge and get into my cart. I can take you up as far as Raleigh, maybe, and I'd leave you with someone who'd send you up farther on the underground road."

"But what about Mama?" I asked. "If we runned off, Master Bricker would take it out on her."

Mama put her arm around me. "If you boys was free," she said, "there wouldn't be nothing Master Bricker could do would hurt me."

"Besides," the Preacher added, "you could fix it so he wouldn't know just what happened to you, whether you runned off, got stolen or drownded or what."

"Can we go, Mama?" begged Obie.

"I got to think some more," she answered uncertainly. "It's so far to go and you're so little." Then turning to the Preacher she asked, "Couldn't you pick them up some place nearer than that bridge?"

He shook his head. "I just can't risk to be in the neighborhood when any slave disappears. If the white folks get to suspecting me, I can't be no more use."

Then he asked me to look outside and see if he could leave without being seen. I told him yes, and then showed him the way along the path to the main road where he had camped for the night.

As we parted he put his hand on my shoulder. "I'll see you, I reckon, July 5th, by the new Pee Dee Bridge."

I trudged slowly back to the cabin. All of a sudden I could feel my head full and ready to burst with new thoughts and my heart with new feelings. Everything seemed strange and dangerous and exciting. A bunch of slaves had got together behind the cabins and were singing, as they often did on Sunday night. Through the dark I heard the words of the spiritual, kind of ringing and haunting:

*"Didn't my Lord deliver Daniel, deliver Daniel,
    deliver Daniel?
Didn't my Lord deliver Daniel, then why not
    every man?"*

2

THE NEXT few weeks were different from any that had gone before. I was doing the same things, mostly hoeing, weeding and watering in the Mistress's vegetable garden or in the cotton fields, but I did it all with a funny new feeling that after thirty, after twenty, after ten, and then at last after one more day I would never work in those fields again. When I talked to one of the other boys I was always remembering that pretty soon he wouldn't see me anymore, and he didn't even know it. And in the evening when I looked around our bare little cabin, and especially when I talked to Mama and Sally, the excitement and adventure got all mixed up with an awful feeling of loss.

I knew that Obie was feeling the same way, and with him everything showed more. Every few days Mama or I would have to warn him about dropping hints, looking at me in a kind of knowing way, or smiling a little bit too mysteriously.

Saturday night, July 2nd, finally came, and as soon as we had cleaned up and eaten, we got everything ready for the next morning. Obie and I set out our fishing poles—we'd decided that two black boys walking away from their master's plantation would look less suspicious if they carried poles. Mama was going to tell the master on Monday night that we'd gone fishing and hadn't come back. That would give him a chance to think that we might have got lost or drownded instead of being sure we'd run off.

Mama packed up some food in a sack for us. The Mistress sometimes gave her eggs for little Sally, and she had saved four of them and hard-boiled them for us. She put in a couple of carrots, too, and a lot of corn bread. After that we all lay down and tried to sleep. It must have been several hours before I dozed off, and then I kept waking up wondering if it was time to get up, but Mama, who was lying on her mattress wide awake, would tell me it was still night. Sometime after midnight I went really to sleep but was soon woken up by Obie shaking my shoulder and whispering excitedly, "Amos, get up, get up. It must be time."

I went out and looked at the sky, but it was still pitch dark. After that none of us slept anymore and finally Mama told us we could get up and dress. She gave us each a big plate of grits she had fixed the night before. She couldn't warm them up because she didn't want anyone to smell the fire so early in the morning. I tried to eat because I knew it would be the last real meal I'd have for two days, but I found that eating was just as hard as sleeping. I felt sick, and every mouthful of cold grits made me feel sicker. Obie was the same, so after urging us for a while, Mama took the plates away.

Then she reached into a box where she kept her few belongings and brought out a small bag of barley sugar candies which she put in our food sack.

"There's a little present I got for you boys," she said.

"How'd you get them, Mama?"

"Remember the Master gave me ten cents when I found his hunting knife just after Christmas?"

We both felt the love behind that present and were kind of stricken. Obie took two candies out of the bag, took them over to Sally and tucked them into her hand.

"That's for you, Sally," he said solemnly, "from me and Amos."

Mama hugged us close and told us to say a prayer before we left. The three of us knelt down there on the dirt floor, and Mama's lips were moving, but no words came, only a kind of strangled sobbing sound. At last she whispered in a broken, almost angry voice, "I can't do no more for them, Lord. You got to help them now."

We got up, took our fishing poles and the sack of food, kissed Mama, and went out the door—for the last time. Obie was crying bitterly—crying for both of us, I guess —as we walked up the path to the road in the early morning light. The sky had already turned from black to gray, and we could hardly see the stars anymore. Once we got to the main road Obie's sobs soon turned to sniffles.

"In four years we'll be almost grown," he said after a while.

"When we get North we can help Pa, and then he'll be able to get Mama sooner," I reminded him.

"Maybe we could get Mama sooner if we wouldn't

ask for Sally at the same time." He sniffed a little bit more hopefully.

"Obie, you know Mama wouldn't never leave Sally all alone." I tried to sound shocked, and didn't let on that I'd had the same idea myself.

"Maybe when we're all together again we can have a little house of our own, a little farm. Maybe we could even get a puppy. . . ."

The sun was slowly rising and our spirits were going up a little bit, too, by the time we got to the woods. Here we left the road and cut over to the stream where we often went fishing. We had already decided to do as much wading as we could in case the Master put dogs on our trail. A slave had run off the year before from a neighboring farm and had been tracked down by a pair of coon hounds.

It was pretty slow going, walking in the stream. The water was running so fast it was hard to keep our balance, and there were lots of twists and turns. As we rounded one especially sharp bend, we stopped in our tracks. There, about fifty feet ahead of us, fishing in the stream, were the Brickers' twin sons, Master Fred and Master Frank. We stared at them and they stared back at us. Then Obie and I started whispering and tugging at each other at the same moment.

He was pulling me back and whispering, "Come on, run."

I was pulling him forward, muttering, "Act natural. Don't run. They already seen us."

But I didn't have the nerve to walk right past them. They were sitting on the right bank, so, clutching firmly onto Obie's shirt, I clambered up the left bank and walked, just as slowly as I could stand to, into the trees. I knew we shouldn't look back, but I just couldn't help it. Master Fred and Master Frank were also whispering and conferring and pointing toward us. We walked on.

"Hey, come here a minute," called a voice behind us. Obie and I looked at each other in despair. The Bricker boys were a couple of years older than me and much

bigger. There was no time to think, so the long habit of doing what we were told decided for us. We turned around, crossed the stream again and stood before them.

"Any luck, Master Fred?" I asked weakly.

"No, we just got here."

There was a long, awkward pause. Then Master Fred went on in a funny, embarrassed way, "Listen, if you won't mention to anyone that you saw us fishing, we'll give you a jam turnover."

Obie's jaw dropped open and I felt all light-headed with relief. Master Frank noticed our surprise.

"Mother doesn't approve of fishing on Sundays," he explained. "A couple of weeks ago someone saw us and it got back to her and there was . . . well, kind of a fuss . . ."

"And we don't want to . . . to worry her again so soon . . ."

"We won't tell a soul," I promised.

"Cross your heart and hope to die, Amos?"

I was surprised they knew my name. The Master and the Mistress never could connect the names with the faces of their slave children.

"Cross my heart and hope to die," I said and Obie repeated.

Then Master Frank opened the picnic box beside him, carefully studied the three jam turnovers, and after deciding which was the smallest, handed it to me. We thanked them with real feeling and set off again across the stream and through the trees. It was all I could do to keep Obie from skipping.

As soon as we were safely out of sight and hearing we sat down to rest our legs and recover a little bit from our scare. Obie wanted to eat the turnover before it got all squashed up.

"You can eat it," I said. "I don't want to take nothing more from the Brickers."

"What d'you mean? Take it. They gave it—kind of like a good-by present."

"Well, I don't want no present from them."

Obie shrugged and took the turnover out of the food bag. I took some bread and turned my back so as not to watch him enjoying it. But I still couldn't help hearing him smack his lips. We never ate anything like that except maybe at Christmas.

"Amos," said Obie after a few bites, "you know that old dry bread come from the Master just as much as this scrumptious turnover."

It was true. I guess he saw that I was wavering.

"Besides, don't you think they owe you a little something after all the weeding you done?"

He broke the turnover into two pieces and held out one to me. So that first meal that we ate in freedom was also the most delicious we'd ever had.

❧ 3

WE GOT to Searsville late in the morning, and I guess most of the people were in church. Anyway the streets were almost empty and we got through without any trouble. We'd never been farther than Searsville before, but Mama had told us to find the Dearborn Creek just north of the town and follow along beside it till it ran into the Pee Dee River. A road ran right next to the creek the first part of the way. By the middle of the afternoon we'd got to another little town. I don't know what its name was because we couldn't read the sign, but it was a bad place for us.

There was a small park right about in the middle of the town with benches along the edge. On the benches sat a row of old men smoking and chewing and sunning themselves, and as we walked toward them they all turned and stared at us. It made me feel fidgety. I shifted my fishing pole from one shoulder to the other, then back again to the first. I glanced at Obie. He looked like a rabbit that's just noticed a hound in front of him.

"Look ordinary," I whispered.

He gave a little start at the sound of my voice, and I said it again.

"Look ordinary."

That was too much for him. "Shut up," he snapped back.

His anger gave me an idea, and I just prayed that he would catch on.

"Gi' me that bag," I yelled, grabbing the food sack. "It's mine."

He gave me kind of a bewildered look, then his face lighted up.

"It's mine," he yelled back.

"'Tisn't."

"'Tis."

"'Tisn't."

By now we had reached the first man in the row of old men, and out of the corner of my eye I saw that he was chuckling.

"'Tis."

"'Tisn't."

At this point Obie snatched the food sack away from me and started running down the street. I took off after him. As I ran, I stole one look at our audience and saw that they were holding their sides with unsuspecting laughter. Obie and I didn't stop running till we were out of town.

That night we spent in a wood, huddled together under some dead leaves. It was cold and scary and lonesome, but at least we could tell each other that we'd walked more than fifteen miles and we hadn't been caught yet.

In the early morning we set off again along the tow-path beside the creek. It was a holiday, July 4th, and there were plenty of fishermen out. After a few miles we sat down and did some fishing ourselves. Obie caught a small one, and a friendly old tramp let us cook it over a fire where he was fixing his own fish. We were glad to get it because there wasn't much left in our food sack. What little there was we finished for lunch, and then we swam across the creek and walked on the other side for a while so as to throw off any dogs that might be set to tracking us.

Swimming with our fishing poles was pretty tricky, and when we crossed back Obie scratched his neck with the hook. It didn't bleed too much, but he got kind of tearful. I just knew he was thinking about Mama and how she would say, "Does it hurt a lot?" and "That's a brave boy," so I tried patting him on the shoulder, telling him, "That's too bad, Obie," but it didn't sound the same. Then I thought the best would be to walk a little ahead and pretend not to hear his sniffs. Pretty soon he perked up again.

A little later we got to the place where the Dearborn Creek ran into the Pee Dee River, and we kept on walking along the river bank. We passed a couple of bridges and were starting to get worried about picking the right one to sit under, but then in the middle of the afternoon we came to one that looked new all over, and we were sure that was our meeting place. There was no path along the river at this point and there were bushes and reeds on both sides of the bridge, so it was a perfect hiding place. At first it scared us to have footsteps and wheels pass right over our heads and to hear voices so close by, but we soon got used to it.

We spent the night there under the bridge and in the morning started listening and watching for the Preacher. We had a long wait. Several carts passed by, and most of them slowed down as they came up to the bridge. Each time we expected to hear the wheels creak to a halt, but each time they would speed up again and cross over.

Once we heard footsteps on the bridge above us along with a patter of paws. The paws stopped short and there was a series of snorting sniffs, then a dog ran back over the bridge, down the bank and through the reeds and stopped a few feet in front of us, barking furiously.

"Custis—drat that dog—come here, Custis," called a man's voice.

Custis, a small, shaggy mutt, paid no attention.

"Custis, come here, darn you."

"Go on, Custis. He's calling you," whispered Obie beseechingly.

The tail was wagging cheerfully now, but the barks were just as accusing as ever.

"All right, stay there, drat you," growled the voice from above, and the footsteps stamped off.

The barking became a little bit uncertain, and in another minute Custis scrambled up the bank and trotted off after his master.

Now there was another sound, the creak and rattle of a cart coming toward the bridge. As usual it slowed down, but then, instead of speeding up again, it pulled to a halt. We saw a dark, stooping figure edging down the bank to the river, carrying a water jug.

"It's Preacher Prentice," whispered Obie, all set to bounce out from our hiding place. But I held him back, remembering that the Preacher would start to sing when our way was clear. The Preacher filled his jug slowly, without ever looking in our direction. A horse's hoofs clattered over the bridge and the rider called down to the Preacher to know whether he was on the right road

for Searsville. Then he galloped off and we strained our ears in the silence.

At last we heard the song: *"Steal away, steal away, steal away to Jesus. Steal away, steal away home . . ."*

Before he had finished the verse we had stolen up the

bank to the waiting wagon. The Preacher had cleared a little space for us behind all his pots and pans. There wasn't room for our fishing poles, so I snuck down the bank again and shoved them under the bridge. When I got back to the wagon Obie was already curled up inside, and I crawled in beside him. The Preacher handed us a bag of hard biscuits and covered us over with a mattress. Then we felt him piling other stuff on top of that. He was humming cheerfully and chuckling to himself as he bustled about, so we knew he was glad we'd come.

Soon we heard him chirping to the horse, and the wagon moved slowly forward over the bridge.

❧ 4

THE WHEELS turned and the hours passed. Obie and I lay hidden under the bedding at the back of the wagon. Sometimes we dozed, sometimes we munched on the biscuits the Preacher had given us, but mostly we just lay there and thought. Today was July 5th. Everyone would be back at work at the Bricker farm, and they would know we were missing. The summer before, Master Bricker's favorite spaniel had gotten lost, and me and Obie and five other boys were taken out of the fields and put to search for him for two days. We knew the Master didn't like us as much as he did that dog, but still we were worth a lot more money to him. Wouldn't he take even more trouble to get us back— borrow hounds, send out descriptions, post rewards?

We got our answer by late afternoon. A couple of horsemen galloped up behind the Preacher's cart and ordered him to stop.

"Where's your pass, boy?" said a gruff voice.

The Preacher explained that he was a freedman, and there was considerable shuffling of papers. Evidently he had some documents to prove it.

"Oh, I know 'bout him," said a second voice. "He's that old tinker. He's harmless. Very religious."

"Well, let's check the cart anyhow. Who knows?"

There was a jangling of pots and pans at the front of the cart.

"What's in that corner, Jim?"

"Bare boards."

I could hear the pounding of my heart even above the rattle of metal.

"Perhaps if you gentlemen would tell me what you're looking for I could help you out," suggested the Preacher mildly.

"We're looking for a couple of little nigger boys from the Bricker place over the other way from Searsville. Bricker's offering twenty-five bucks a head reward for them."

The searching hands were getting closer. I thought wildly of jumping up and running for it, but I was too numb with fear even to move.

"Kind of ugly-looking youngsters?" inquired the Preacher.

"It don't say." There was a pause in the search. "Says here they're twelve and nine, short, thin, very dark skin, long narrow heads, big eyes. Don't say if they're ugly."

The rattling of pans started up again, right above my foot this time.

"Did they have fishing poles?"

Another pause.

"Why, yes, they must have had. They was last seen going fishing."

"Check under that mattress, Jim."

"Well, what d'you know. That must've been them," mused the Preacher, as if to himself.

Jim never moved the mattress that was covering Obie and me.

"What must've been them?"

"Why, I saw a couple of youngsters would fit that description just this morning."

"Where?" Both voices sang out together.

"You know that new bridge over the Pee Dee River?"

"Where the road turns?"

"Yes. There was two kids with fishing poles sitting under that bridge this morning. Looked like they could be hiding."

"How long ago?"

"Some hours. I don't have no way to tell the time real exact."

"Come on, Jim. Don't stand there talking. They might still be there."

"Good day to you, gentlemen," said the Preacher, but there was no answer. The two were already galloping down the road. We just lay quiet for a while, still weak with fear.

The Preacher soon pulled off the road at a shady spot.

"Well, well, it's been a mighty hot day for an old fellow like me," he chortled.

Obie crawled out from under the bedding. "Oh, Preacher Prentice, I just wouldn't have believed that anyone could be that clever. And they said you was harmless!"

"Harmless as doves and wise as serpents. That's what the Lord told us to be, and I do my best," chuckled the Preacher.

"And the good part is when they get back to the bridge they'll find our fishing poles, and they'll think you was telling the truth."

"For me the good part is that I was telling the truth." He was speaking very quietly and seriously now. "I have told lies, and I would tell 'em again if it's for someone's freedom, but . . . but . . . well, I don't lie easy."

"What if someone else comes to search the wagon?"

"Well, I'll tell you what. I was trying to get out of this area as fast as the old hoss could pull us and not stopping for nothing. But now I reckon it'll be safer to stop in at some of the plantations roundabout and do some tinkering. We ain't more than three miles from Judge Witherspoon's place, and I doubt anyone would go there to look for runaway slaves. Giddy up, old boy."

We spent the next seven days at the back of that wagon. The Preacher made a lot of stops at the farms along the way to sell or fix pots and pans, and sometimes in the evening he would lead a prayer meeting. Slaves weren't supposed to have any kind of gathering by themselves, and once in a while a master or an overseer would come to make sure there wasn't too much talk about Moses or Pharaoh or such things, but mostly the white folks didn't bother themselves or us very much. They considered the Preacher quite reliable and probably thought he was having a good influence on their slaves.

We got to Raleigh on a Tuesday afternoon—it must have been July 12th. Obie and I had never seen a real town before, and the Preacher let us come out from our hiding place to look. After winding through the streets for a while he pulled to a stop in a little back alley.

"You wait here while I go talk to the Strausses," he said.

The Preacher had told us about the Strausses the night before. We knew that they were an old couple who had come over from Europe years ago. He told us that they had wanted freedom in their own country, and had worked for it and even fought for it. That kind of people often gets into trouble, and they had. They had had to leave their country and come to America. Now they ran a pharmacy in Raleigh. But they still kept on worrying about freedom, so they had become "brakemen" on the underground railroad.

Now the door opened and the Preacher came out, followed by an elderly white man.

"Ver is ze children?" he asked.

We climbed out of the wagon.

"Good-by, Amos. Good-by, Obadiah. Be good boys, and God bless you." The Preacher gave us each a pat on the head.

We had known, of course, that he would leave us in Raleigh, but we hadn't known how bad we'd feel. He was the last link with our old life, with Mama and Sally and the cabin, and he was going away. I tried to think of something to say that would make him stay a little longer, but I couldn't think of anything at all. I didn't even remember to say thank you, but just gulped, muttered "Good-by," and followed Mr. Strauss and Obie through the back door.

❧ 5

MR. AND MRS. STRAUSS looked very much alike. They were both small, frail-looking and gray-haired, but they didn't seem old or tired. It's hard to really explain, but their wrinkled faces seemed kind of transparent. In some funny way they made me think of the beat-up hurricane lamp in the Brickers' barn; you hardly noticed the chips and cracks in its chimney when you saw the bright flame inside.

They lived in two small rooms over the pharmacy with little furniture but a lot of books. We had never been in a white person's house before, except once in a while in the Brickers' kitchen, and at first we felt mighty strange and uncomfortable. The Strausses must have understood our feeling, because they did everything they could to make us welcome. Whenever they could get away from their customers one or the other would come up the stairs to us, bringing something nice to eat or some game or trick to entertain us. They even let me look at one of the books with very fancy, exciting pictures in it. I knew they were being kind, but I just kept wishing

they would go back to the store and leave us to ourselves.

In the evening when the store was closed Mr. Strauss unfolded a big sheet of paper all covered with lines and markings, and began to pore over it, muttering names like "Zearsville," "Richmond," "Vashington," and "Phila-delphia."

Obie, always curious, asked, "What's that, Master Strauss?"

"Zat, my boy, is a map. Zat is a picture of ver you have been and ver you must go."

Obie and I crowded around him.

"Raleigh is here and zer is Philadelphia. Zer you must go."

"But that isn't very far at all, Master Strauss. We can do that real quick," exclaimed Obie. "Where did we come from?"

"Hm, let me zee. Zis village Zearsville, it is here. Just over ze line in Sout Carolina."

Obie's face fell. "But we been gone more than a week. We got to be farther than that."

Mr. Strauss chuckled. "Everything is small on ze map. You have come about hundred miles, more or less. You must go still—let me zee—two hundred zixty to Vashington, to Philadelphia must be about four hundred miles."

That sounded like a long, long way.

"But now," continued Mr. Strauss, "ve shall plot only ze next step. Ve must get you here, to Dr. Culpepper in Henderson. Do you know your letters, my boys?"

"I know *B*," said Obie proudly. "That's the first letter in Bricker and it's on the sign on his driveway. Amos knows more than me, though. Pa started to teach him before they took him away."

"He just taught me a few, and I forgot them pretty well," I admitted.

"Zat is a great trouble. How to find ze way when you cannot read ze sign and you cannot ask ze people. Vell, ve must tink."

He scratched his head, wrinkled up his forehead and talked for a while to his wife in some queer foreign language. Then he turned to us and switched back to English.

"Ve have ze plot," he announced. "You must go by day. At night you shall be lost. You ver sent to Raleigh by Dr. Culpepper to try if any pharmacy has a certain new medicine. You found it at my store and now you take it back to him. You have lost your pass, but I shall give you a letter to ze doctor zat you can show if somebody shall stop you. I shall give you a little map also."

"Only vun ting," added Mrs. Strauss. "Ven you come near Henderson, so if anybody ask, you do not belong to Dr. Culpepper. Many zere shall know zat he have no slaves. Say zat you belong to Mr. Strauss and he send you with medicine zat ze doctor ordered."

"If zey ask vy ve do not use ze mail, say ve are foreigners—how do you say—eccentric, and you can still show ze letter."

The rest of the evening was spent in preparations. Mrs. Strauss filled a large medicine jar with red candy and pasted labels and warnings all over it while Mr. Strauss wrote his letter. Then they both went over the route to Henderson with us. It was a distance of about thirty miles, and they expected it to take us two days. They wrote down the names of some of the places we would pass on the way and we tried to memorize them.

Then Mrs. Strauss glanced up at the clock.

"Ach! It is eight and a half. You children shall sleep here on ze sofa. I get a blanket."

It was a hot night and we soon kicked off the blanket,

but late at night I heard Mrs. Strauss tiptoe in and I felt her tucking the blanket around my shoulders. I almost thought I was back in the cabin with Mama, and all of a sudden I wanted to cry.

The Strausses were up before us in the morning. Mrs. Strauss had made us a big breakfast of eggs and sausages and had stuffed our food sack. Mr. Strauss was once again checking the "pill" jar, the letter and the map. At last all was ready. We said good-by and set off.

That morning I felt for the first time the joy and excitement of the road. The sun was bright and the air warm and soft. The country was green and rolling, and my heart was all grateful and full of hope. Obie whistled as he walked along beside me, and I knew he felt the same.

We were stopped once on the edge of town by a well-dressed young white man. We told him we were buying medicine for our master, and when he had looked at the pills and read Mr. Strauss's letter he shrugged his shoulders and went on his way.

About five miles along the road we were stopped again, this time by a rough-looking man in a farm cart.

"Hey, you little coons, where d'you think you're going?"

We told the story about the medicine again and showed him the letter. He read it out loud to himself, slowly sounding out the words and following them with a grubby finger:

"Dear Dr. Culpepper, I send the medicine requested by you with these boys. It is already widely used in Europe but difficult to obtain in this country. I would advise a dosage of two pills before breakfast and one before bed. Please inform me of the progress of your patient. Your obedient servant, Joseph Strauss."

He handed back the letter.

"Wonder what that there medicine's good for?"

"Sciatica," answered Obie off the top of his head.

"Sciatica, eh? That's what my old lady complains of. Maybe I'll get some of them pills next time I'm in town."

He started up again, then stopped.

"Where'd you say your master lives—Henderson?"

"Yes, sir."

"Well, jump in the back. I'm going up that way about fourteen miles and I'll give you a lift."

The more you got to know our driver the nicer he seemed to get. By the time he let us off in the middle of the afternoon, we had talked over his wife's sciatica, the awful cost of medicine, the cleverness of his horse, and a lot of other things, and we felt pretty friendly. When we separated he gave us each a stick of licorice. Right away Obie dug into his pocket and fished out a handful of candy that Mrs. Strauss had given him to offer in return. To my horror I saw that it was the same round, red candy that was shining out from the medicine jar. Luckily, our friend wasn't a very noticing person. Or what he noticed was the wrong thing—my face.

"Naw," he told Obie. "You're going to be in trouble with your big brother if you give me any of that candy. Thanks anyway." And he turned into a side road and drove off.

We were only about eleven miles from Henderson now and well rested, with several hours of daylight still ahead of us, so we decided to try to walk straight through without stopping for the night. We made it, too, though we had to walk the last few miles in the dark. Those last miles were the hardest and slowest. Every sound frightened us, and even the trees, hills and bushes seemed alive and unfriendly. At last we saw the dim shapes of the town ahead of us. By the time we walked down the main street many of the lights were already in upper windows, and in some houses there was no light at all. We carefully followed the Strausses' directions through the town until we came to a large white frame house with a fence around it. By the light of the full moon we were just able to make out the letters on the gate. They spelled out the name we had memorized the night before: Culpepper.

✤ 6

WE WENT around to the back door and knocked softly. There was no sound from the dark house. We knocked again louder. There was some movement inside, and a sleepy voice called, "Coming." In a minute the door was opened by a pleasant-faced middle-aged gentleman holding a candle. Even in his nightcap he looked dignified.

"What is it, my lads? Who sent you?" he asked.

"Dr. Culpepper?"

"I am he."

"Master Strauss sent us. We're going north."

The doctor looked at us blankly for a moment; then a light dawned.

"Surely you're not alone?" he inquired, peering into the darkness behind us.

"Yes, sir. There's just us."

"Well, come in and welcome," said the doctor.

Once inside he searched about in the larder and soon had two plates of cold meat before us. While we ate he asked us questions and we told him our story. I could see that he was surprised and concerned at our traveling so far alone.

After we had eaten he led us up the back stairs to a small guest room.

"Sleep as late as you wish in the morning," he told us. "You'll have to get used to sleeping during the day and traveling at night."

That night for the first time in our lives we slept between sheets. I can still remember how clean and smooth and rich they felt.

We did sleep late the next morning, and when we finally got up the doctor was already at work in his consulting room. As we soon found out, he was a widower with five daughters, the eldest already a young lady and the youngest a little older than me. The father was a quiet, plain-looking man, but the girls were all lively and pretty, with long yellow hair and long, pretty names: Melissa, Belinda, Veronica, Amelia and Christina.

They made a big fuss over us, brought us nice things to eat, and fixed up some clothes of the cook's children for us, as our own were getting tattered and dirty. We each got an extra pair of pants and a shirt, even underclothes, which we'd never worn before. Then Miss Belinda made us each stand on a piece of paper while she drew a line around our feet. We thought it was some kind of game until she said she was going to send the coachman out to buy shoes for us. Obie thought shoes might be fun, but I shushed him up and told her no, trying not to sound ungrateful or hurt her feelings. We'd been walking and working barefoot all our lives and had never had any trouble, but I remembered how little Billy,

one of the boys back home, had tried to wear some old
cast-off shoes of Master Frank's and had got his feet all
covered with blisters.

When the girls weren't working over us they were
entertaining us. They taught Obie to play a duet on

the piano and to paint with water colors and to make a cat's cradle. I felt too shy and awkward to do things like that, but it was fun just to stand around and watch. After a while Miss Melissa, the oldest, asked if there wasn't anything I would like to do, and I plucked up all my courage and told her I would like to learn to read. She didn't seem too surprised, but found up an old copybook and took me downstairs to the parlor. There she explained the sounds of the different letters to me, and wrote some words, and whenever I figured one out she was almost as excited as I was. We were just going over *dog*, and *log*, and *hog*, when the front door bell rang.

"It must be for Papa," said Miss Melissa, shoving the copybook under a cushion. "But you'd better get under the sofa just in case."

As I started to wriggle and slither into my hiding place I saw the maid pass by, hurrying to open the door. The sofa was very low set and its springs must have been worn. The whole weight of Miss Melissa's body seemed to be squashing down on my feet, which had to be turned sideways in a terribly uncomfortable position. I got a glimpse of the maid's feet beneath the ruffle of the sofa.

"It's Mr. Edgar Simpson and he wants to speak with you, Miss Melissa," she said nervously.

"Edgar? Very well. Would you please just go upstairs, Nellie, and tell my sister that Obadiah must be kept absolutely quiet for a while."

"Yes, miss."

A moment later a pair of highly polished black boots came into the room.

"Edgar, what can bring you so early in the afternoon? Sit down."

He did, and a great weight settled itself squarely on my nose. It was all I could do to hold back a grunt of pain.

"Dearest, I have such exciting news. I simply had to leave the office and come and tell you. Do you remember last week I told you we had an important inheritance case? Well, this morning the client came in again and asked that I be put in charge of it. He said he wanted an energetic young man to represent him and he liked my approach. I'll leave for Philadelphia the day after tomorrow, and Mr. Andrews has promised that if I handle the case well, I shall be made a partner, and then, Melissa . . ."

"Oh, Edgar!"

"We can . . . we can set the date."

The pressure shifted from my nose to my stomach as Edgar edged closer to his sweetheart.

"You're always so clever, Edgar. I know you'll handle it beautifully."

"If I don't it won't be for lack of trying."

"Did you say Philadelphia, Edgar?" Miss Melissa asked thoughtfully.

"Yes. I hate the thought of being so far from you, dearest, but it'll only be for about two months."

"How will you go?"

I knew that she and I were thinking about the same thing.

"I'll take the carriage, I suppose."

There was a long pause. Finally Miss Melissa spoke:

"Edgar, you do agree with Papa on the question of slavery, don't you?"

He sounded pretty taken aback as he answered: "Well, I believe so, but really, what . . ." That certainly was not the question he had come to talk about.

"I know the whereabouts of two runaway slaves, Edgar. They are trying to get to Philadelphia. If they could go with you . . ."

A heavy silence again. I held my breath as I waited for the answer. Then the young man spoke, slowly, as if he were trying to figure out the meaning of his own words.

"You know the whereabouts of two runaway slaves? You're trying to help them?"

"Yes, Edgar."

"Melissa, I can hardly believe it. What would your father say if he knew?" He sounded mighty shocked.

He does know. He's hiding them.

"Your father . . . But he's a born Southerner, a . . . a gentleman, a . . . a . . . a vestryman. He's . . . he's not the kind of person to do that."

"Well, he must be, because he does it," replied Miss Melissa simply.

The young man spoke now in a kind of scared whisper. "Melissa, doesn't he know the penalties for slave-stealing? He could spend the rest of his life in prison. There'd be ruinous fines, and the whole family would be disgraced."

"How can you talk about slave-stealing?" she answered fiercely. "Papa wants no slaves. He freed all his own. Why would he steal them from someone else?"

"Helping them escape or stealing them, it's all the same in the eyes of the law. It's depriving someone of his property. You've heard of the Charles Torrey case, that Northern minister who was caught a few years ago. He died in prison and left his family destitute. And there was a sea captain I read about. He was not only imprisoned but branded, and . . ."

"Edgar, you know Papa. No amount of imprisonment or fines would prevent him from doing what he thinks is right."

"But it's not right," Edgar almost shouted. "It's breaking the law."

"Papa thinks the law is unjust."

"He thinks—that's just it. Justice has to be a matter of opinion, but law is a fact. I happen to agree with your father and disagree with the law. But if one could simply disobey any law he disagreed with, then the law would be finished. After all, some people dislike the laws you think are just."

"But what can you do if the law tells you to do something you're sure is wrong, or not to do something you're sure is right? What can you do then?"

"Change the law." He pounded the arm of the sofa. "Don't break it, change it. And it will be changed—I know it will. I'm absolutely certain that in fifty years slavery will be a thing of the past."

He sounded so earnest and well intentioned as he said it that I almost wanted to come out from my hiding place and explain to him that I had only one life, on this earth anyway, and in fifty years it would be mostly over. But he went on in a gentler tone:

"I know how you feel about it, Melissa. Believe me I do. You know my father contributes every Christmas to the American Colonization Society, and when . . ."

He stopped short as another set of footsteps sounded in the hall.

"Oh! Good afternoon, Dr. Culpepper," and a great weight was lifted from my stomach as he rose to his feet.

"Good afternoon, Edgar. What can be causing you to neglect the law at this hour?"

"Well, sir, as a matter of fact I was just about to leave." He sounded confused and embarrassed. "I had just stopped in to tell Melissa some news and I must get back to the office. Good-by—I'll stop in again tomorrow evening."

The polished black boots marched out of the room and the front door creaked open and then slammed shut.

"You and Edgar have not been quarreling, I trust?" inquired the doctor.

"Oh, Papa! I told him about hiding those little boys and helping the underground railroad."

"That was a very foolish thing to do, my dear. As long as those children are in our home we have a grave responsibility for their safety."

"He thinks one should never, never break the law."

"A very appropriate attitude in a lawyer."

"Oh, Papa! Please don't joke." I could just about hear the tears in her voice. "He says it's wrong to ever break the law."

"I'm not joking, Melissa. That's what your dear mother used to say."

He was silent for a minute and I could almost feel him

groping for words. Then he went on, slowly and with an effort.

"You know, I think that I have never broken the law lightly or in my own interest. But the laws of North Carolina are not the only ones by which I am obligated..."

There was something in his tone that made me remember the way the Preacher had talked about telling lies, and I thought how mixed up and difficult things can get for a person who really cares about doing right.

"Oh, dear!" said Miss Melissa. "I really agree with both of you at the same time, but I suppose that's impossible. It makes my head ache just to think about it."

"Well, these questions have addled better heads than ours," replied the doctor. "So let's get back to more practical matters and make arrangements for tonight. Where are the boys?"

"I'm right here, sir," I answered, sticking my head out from under the sofa.

"Oh, Amos! I'd quite forgotten you," cried Miss Melissa.

The doctor laughed. "Well, my boy, you've heard all about the philosophy of your escape. Now you must study the geography of it. Fetch your brother."

I got Obie, and the doctor showed us the next part of our route on the map.

"I'll take you as far as South Hill in Virginia in the carriage tonight," he explained. "From there . . ."

"But, Papa," interrupted Miss Melissa, "that's about thirty miles. You won't be home till morning, and you look tired already. Why not let John drive them? He's perfectly reliable."

"John will drive them, and I shall nap in the carriage. I told John to have a rest this afternoon, so he will be fresh."

The doctor told us we must travel on to the next station by night. He told us to stay close to the road, but to hide every time we heard footsteps or hoofbeats.

There might be patrols on the road. Our next station would be a tannery about fifteen miles north of South Hill. It belonged to a Quaker named Elijah McNaul.

"McNaul is a bachelor and lives in a boardinghouse," explained the doctor. "Of course he can't hide you there, and there are a couple of other men working for him in the tannery. So this is what you must do. He keeps a very large box out behind the back door. Open it up and get in. There'll be plenty of room for you both. McNaul always checks that box first thing when he comes to work in the morning, and he'll have you fed and bedded down in the loft before his employees arrive. Now go to the kitchen, boys. I told Nellie to prepare you an early supper."

The girls came out to the kitchen with us and while we ate they stuffed all kinds of nice things into our food sack. They put in a candle, and matches too, but warned us not to light it in the dark unless we really had to.

It must have been about six o'clock in the evening when we finally set off. Obie and I lay on the floor; John, the coachman, sat on his box, grumbling to himself, and the doctor looked out the carriage window and bowed to his neighbors as we passed. As soon as it grew dark he let us look out the windows while he dozed. It was nice to watch the big dark shapes slipping by in the night and to think of the miles slipping by with them. As it got later Obie and I got drowsier and drowsier until we were awakened by a sudden shout.

"Dr. Culpepper! Stop! Dr. Culpepper!"

We dived down to the floor of the carriage, while John, instead of stopping, whipped up the horses. Dr. Culpepper opened his eyes.

"Stop, John," he ordered.

The carriage stopped and a man ran up behind us swinging a lantern.

"Dr. Culpepper, is it you?"

"Yes. Evans?"

"Yes, Doc. It's me. Thank the Lord I met you. My Bessie's real bad. She's having a rough delivery. I was just going for help. Can you come?"

"Just pull off the road, John, and wait here," said the doctor as he got out of the carriage and followed Evans.

In about half an hour he was back.

"How's the baby?" asked John.

"What baby?" The doctor laughed. "It's a fine, healthy calf. Bessie is Evans' cow, not his wife."

"That scoundrel," growled John. "I reckon he still owes you for his last three kids, and now he expects you to deliver his calves, too. You shouldn't do it, Doctor."

"Well, well," said the doctor mildly, "it would hardly be fair to punish the cow for her owner's omissions. Now let's be on our way again."

The next time I woke up the carriage was stopped again. The doctor told us that we were now in Virginia, just past South Hill, and that he must now turn back.

" 'Bout time, too," muttered John.

The doctor wished us well and pointed out the road we should follow. When we started to thank him he seemed embarrassed and said he must be off. Soon the wheels were rolling away again and Obie and I were left alone in the darkness.

7

WE WALKED on until the sun rose, then spent the day hiding and sleeping in the tall grass of a swamp, and the next evening we went on again. Walking in the dark was scary and awful. We were afraid to walk on the road for fear of being seen, so we went along beside it and were always walking into puddles or briars, or stubbing our bare toes against roots or stones. Many times we thought we heard horses coming toward us, and sometimes we really did. Then we would lie flat on the earth, hold our breaths and pray silently till the danger passed. Many times, as we passed farmhouses in the night, dogs would bark a warning to their owners. Many times we startled rabbits and foxes and flocks of wood pigeons, and they startled us. Once I stepped on a snake, but in my terror I jumped away before it could bite me.

The only thing that helped at all was Obie. I knew that he was just as scared as me—maybe more, because he was younger. But he never let on. He tried to talk about cheerful things like the angels that maybe were watching out for us, or how close we must be getting to the

McNaul tannery, or about things that would take our minds off the darkness, like how smart the Preacher was, how nice the Strausses were, and why such an ordinary-seeming person as Dr. Culpepper would be helping the underground railroad. And just seeing how much he wanted to make me feel better did make me feel better.

The second night was almost over, and Obie had just said for about the fifteenth time that we must be almost at the village where the tannery was, when we saw the houses of the village before us. We tiptoed down the deserted main street till we came to a large building set back from the road with a big round sign swinging out in front of it. We knew from Dr. Culpepper's description that this was the tannery. Safety at last! We went around to the back and carefully lighted the candle to look for the box. There it was, just as the doctor had said. I was just pushing up the lid and starting to climb in when I looked down. There was a pair of eyes, wild with terror, staring up at me. A scream started in my throat, but just as in a bad dream it stayed there. I couldn't make a sound. I froze. I felt a pair of strong hands closing around my neck. I tried again to scream, but all that came was a kind of strangled gargle. My head felt as if it was about to burst, but I realized dimly that Obie was pulling and punching at the arms that held me. I think I heard a low screech just as I passed out.

When I came to again Obie was bending over me with the candle. A teen-age Negro boy was glaring out of the box at us, nursing an obviously painful bite on his wrist.

"Amos, you all right, Amos?" whispered Obie.

"I think so," I answered unsteadily.

"What you doing here?" snarled the boy in the box. He looked at Obie and then back at his bleeding wrist.

"We was told to come here, and we came," said Obie firmly. "Move over."

"Git out of here," started our friend from the box, but

he suddenly changed his mind as we heard voices and footsteps approaching. "Quick. Git in."

We scrambled into the box and softly closed the lid on ourselves.

"Aw, you just probably had a bad dream," drawled a sleepy voice from outside. "Or maybe it was a couple of tomcats."

"It wasn't no dream. I wasn't even asleep."

"Well, so look here. Where's your burglars? The door's locked and the lock ain't touched."

"Well, I heard it. I heard some scuffling and yelling. I know I did," said the second voice stubbornly.

"You reckon burglars scuffle and yell when they're getting set to pick a lock?"

"So maybe it weren't burglars. You know I suspicioned before that McNaul might be hiding niggers in this here place."

"Yuk, you got too much imagination—that's your trouble. McNaul may be a little bit screwy, but he ain't no criminal."

"He's a Quaker, ain't he?"

"So what? McNaul's snoring away peacefully in his bed right now, and I would be too if it weren't for your dang-blasted imagination." And the speaker stomped off.

"Well, I don't care. I know I heard something and it weren't no cats. It might have been . . ." The voice trailed off around the corner of the building.

It was ten minutes before any of us in the box dared speak. Then Obie broke the silence.

"My name's Obadiah."

There was a grunt from the other end of the box.

"My brother's name is Amos."

Another grunt. Then silence.

"What's your name?"

"Joe. Now git out."

I started to raise the lid of the box: I was remembering those powerful hands around my neck. But Obie stayed put.

"If we get out, we won't know where to go, and we'll get caught."

A sneer from the other side of the box said, plainly as words, "Who cares?"

"If we get caught," went on Obie, "first thing they're going to ask is if we know where there's some more runaway slaves. That'll be the first thing."

Maybe this thought convinced Joe. He didn't say anything more about our getting out; in fact, he didn't say anything more at all. He just sat there, and though I couldn't see anything in the dark I could feel his eyes turned toward us in fear and hatred.

It seemed hours before the lid was opened from the outside and we blinked up at a strong tanned face surrounded by black curly hair. The man blinked back at us and then said in a solemn tone: "Welcome, pilgrims."

We didn't know the word "pilgrims" then, but it had an important sound.

" 'Scuse me, sir," I ventured. "You Master McNaul?"

"I am Elijah McNaul. No master. Never let me hear that awful word." And he pounded his big brawny fist into his palm. We were all a little shaken by this outburst.

"Yes, Master McNaul," Joe and I whispered together.

"No, Mister McNaul," said Obie.

Our host studied us gloomily for a moment, then nodded at Obie.

"Thee, at least, has some stuffing in thy head," he remarked. "Come in, all three."

We followed him into the tannery and up a ladder into the loft. In spite of his strange manner we soon saw that our host was a good-hearted man. He brought us a breakfast of cold potatoes and ham, blankets which we did not need, and a candle. As we ate I got a good look at Joe for the first time. He seemed to be about seventeen or eighteen years old, not tall but very tough and wiry. He had a very distinctive kind of face, with wide cheeks, a pointed chin and a flattish nose. A long, ugly scar ran from the corner of his eye to his lower jaw.

"What did you do to your face, Joe?" asked Obie as we ate.

"Didn't do nothing to it. The Master did."

"He must be a mean, nasty person."

"A devil! They're all devils." Joe almost spat out the words.

"Master Bricker wasn't no devil." Obie shook his head thoughtfully. "He was pretty stingy about buying things, but he wasn't no devil. One of the girls that worked in the kitchen, she said he was pretty nice sometimes."

"But he was unfair to think that us, and our whole lives and all, it was just something for him . . ." I knew what I wanted to say, but I didn't know how to say it.

"Right, boy. Unfair. Unjust. Blasphemous." Mr. McNaul appeared through the trapdoor carrying a jug of apple juice and spilling some of it in his indignation. "To use a man, made in the image of God, like a . . . like a thing, that's blasphemy. Blasphemy."

Joe signaled us to stop talking. I could see that he trusted this white man even less than he trusted us. But Obie is a hard person to shut up.

"Well, I know it. But maybe Master Bricker don't know. He probably never even thought. He was just born a slave owner, like we was born slaves."

"Dr. Culpepper was born a slave owner, too," I reminded him. "I heard Miss Melissa say so. But he ain't no more."

"Will thee drink some apple juice?" offered Mr. McNaul. "Finish breakfast now, or my men will be here. Finish quickly and blow out the candle. I'll send the men home early today anyway because it's Seventh Day. Then we'll look at the map."

Obie and I went over to one corner of the loft and stretched out, and Joe went over to the opposite corner. The aching tiredness in my legs and the fear from the night before were just beginning to slip away and I felt myself dozing off when a sudden noise jolted me awake. I sat up and peered into the darkness. There it was again: a snort, followed by a whistle, from the other side of the loft. Joe was snoring. I groped my way across the floor toward the corner where he lay, trying not to make a sound. Before I could reach him there was another resounding snort and whistle. I wondered if Mr. McNaul's men had gotten to work yet. A third snore, but right in front of me now. I reached out and touched a body. I poked it. Poor Joe almost jumped out of his skin.

"Joe, you was snoring," I whispered.

He only grunted. Just then we heard the door of the tannery open.

"Thee's early," greeted Mr. McNaul's voice. "Tom's not here yet."

I breathed a sigh of relief. Neither of the workmen had been in time to hear Joe's snores, but I didn't dare return to my own corner in case they started again. I lay down beside him, ready to pounce at the smallest noise. He had had quite a scare too, and it was a while before he went to sleep again. Then the snoring started, but this time I caught him in the middle of the first snort.

"Joe, they'll hear you. They'll catch us all," I whispered.

"I just cain't stay awake. I been running three days."

We both lay there racking our brains.

"Put some blankets over your head," I suggested.

We crept and felt our way around the loft until we found the blankets. Then we wrapped them, layer after layer, around Joe's head. I wondered if his breathing wasn't going to be smothered along with his snores. I stretched out again and waited. Pretty soon there was a muffled noise, then another. Joe was snoring, but no one except me would be able to hear him. I closed my eyes and settled down for a long day's sleep.

❦ 8

WHEN WE set off again that evening Joe was with us. None of us wanted to travel together—he didn't like us and we were afraid of him—but since we were going the same route it seemed the most sensible thing to do.

We rode the first seven miles in Mr. McNaul's wagon under a pile of hides. Then he let us out and we were on our own. Our next station was the home of a lady piano teacher, a Miss Holkum, in Petersburg. Petersburg was about forty miles north, so we had a long walk ahead of us.

Joe walked mighty fast and didn't want to stop for rests as often as we did. We kept asking him to slow down, but he didn't pay any attention. We wouldn't have cared so much about staying with him except that he was carrying our food sack, which was now stuffed with a smoked sausage and cheese besides the usual bread. By morning Obie and I were both tired out and in a bad mood with Joe for pushing us so hard. To make things worse we'd both got some poison ivy around our ankles, and the itching made it hard to rest. Obie scratched his with his fingers, and so he soon had puffy eyes and an itchy chin too. I was more careful and always used a stick or stone to scratch.

The next day got terribly hot and our cheese got all sticky and melty so we decided to eat it right away. At least it was kind of a good feeling to lie in the shade and remember that if we'd been on the Bricker farm we'd have been out working in the sun.

That evening Obie was really miserable with his poison ivy, and he muttered to me that he wasn't going to knock himself out running after Joe. So when we'd walked a couple of miles, Obie said he was going to have a rest and sat down. Joe kept right on walking, and I didn't know what to do. I watched Joe's dim shape moving off into the dark. Then he stopped, and sat down too, a hundred feet ahead of us. After that we took rests whenever we needed them, and sometimes Joe even sat down beside us.

The next morning we settled down for the day in the underbrush beside a pond. The poison ivy was stinging instead of itching, and that didn't bother us so much. We finished off the sausage and noticed that the bread was turning greenish. Joe said that was all right because mold is strengthening, but Obie and I tried to scrape it off when he wasn't looking.

In the evening before we set off Obie told us he was going to get us some honey for our bread. He'd seen what he thought was a beehive in a tree and he went up to get it. But all he got was two wasp stingers in his face and a bruise on his behind when he fell out of the tree again. I guess that was the only time I ever heard Joe laugh.

Joe was luckier at finding food, though. Later on that same evening he saw a striped snake and smashed its head with a rock. We still had some matches that the Culpeppers had given us and a knife that Mr. McNaul had put in with the sausage, so we made a fire, cut up the snake and cooked it. The meat was pretty good, but we were all so worried that someone might notice our fire that we couldn't enjoy it very much.

By the time the sun had risen on the third morning we were still a mile or so outside Petersburg, and we didn't dare walk into town in the daylight. So we spent the day in an empty old shed on the edge of the town and then made our way to Miss Holkum's big, spooky-looking house just after dark. We knocked softly at the back door. It opened just a crack and the frightened, tear-stained face of a Negro woman looked out at us.

"What d'you boys want?"

"Is this Miss Holkum's place?"

"Yes, but she's sick, bad sick."

"We're going north. We was told to come here."

The woman shook her head sadly. "I wish I could help you. I'm Miss Holkum's cook, and we always help, her and me. But I can't let nobody in now. It's typhoid and it's awful catchy. Even the doctor won't hardly come. You just got to keep going till Richmond, till Reverend Pringle's house. That's the next station and it's only twenty-some miles."

Luckily, she knew the way as well as her mistress and explained to us how to get to the Reverend Calvin Pringle's house in Richmond.

Obie dangled our empty food sack. "We don't got no more food," he muttered. "Maybe, maybe . . ."

"Miss Holkum never let nobody leave her place hungry," said the woman. "I'll give you what I got, but it ain't much. I hardly left her bedside these three days, even to go to the store."

She went away and came back with half a loaf of bread.

"It's all we can spare," she said as she handed it to us. She watched as we tiptoed down the back path. We'd got just a few steps when Obie turned back.

"Tell Miss Holkum I sure do wish she gets well," he said.

For the first time the woman tried to smile. "Bless you, child," she answered and shut the door.

We walked all that night and by the next morning we were tired and hungry. Our feet hurt, and Obie had a very sore blister on one sole. Our food sack was empty except for the half loaf of bread, so we'd had to lose some time scrounging for nuts and berries. We also sometimes helped ourselves to fruit from the orchards we passed. That morning the sky was cloudy and it had started to drizzle, and we all felt pretty low.

Every time we'd stop for a rest Obie would start pestering Joe with questions. He never got more than a nod or shake of the head, usually just a growl, but he kept right on trying. That morning, as we lay down under a tree hoping to stay dry, he started in again.

"Joe, was you born at your master's place?"

It didn't seem like a very promising opener, and all it got by way of an answer was a grunt that sounded more like "no" than "yes."

"Then where was you born?" Obie went on.

"Africa."

Obie and I both sat up and gazed at him wide-eyed. "You kidding us, Joe?"

"I was born in Africa," he answered slowly, proudly. Then turning on Obie: "Now don't ask me how'd I come to leave. I didn't choose."

"Then how d'you come to leave, Joe?"

I kind of expected Joe to explode, but he just lay there, staring up through the dripping branches into the dull gray sky. Then he started to talk in a funny, strangled voice.

"It was when I was a little kid—maybe four or five, I don't know. They was fighting around our village and they catched my mother and the baby, but me and my father, we got away. But they was keeping my mother and the other people not so far away, and I wanted her so bad, so I snuck over and . . ."

"That wasn't very smart," Obie interrupted.

"You tell me now?" Joe snarled back. "Well, so they catched me too. They made us walk several days over to some town on the coast and they traded us to the white folks. The white folks, they put us on this boat—we was all chained up down in the middle of the boat. They didn't want no one to see us—there was some law or something—anyway they kept us down there in the middle of the boat, and it was always dark and it stunk something awful. The baby he was crying all the time 'cause my mother couldn't feed him, and then after a while he stopped crying and he was dead. My mother didn't want the white folks to know he was dead. She didn't want them to take him away, but after a while they saw and they took him. Lots of people got sick and died, and then my mother died, too, and the white folks took her away . . ."

His voice trailed off and he lay there staring up into the sky. Then he turned on Obie. "What you got to ask so many questions for? Why cain't you leave me be?"

You could hear how angry he was, but now we figured it wasn't especially at us.

It drizzled and dripped all day and by the time we set out in the evening there was thunder and lightning and it was pouring cats and dogs. After a few hours of plodding through mud and puddles we came to a signpost. I studied it, but I couldn't make out anything in the darkness. When I was just turning away there was a flash of lightning and I saw a lot of letters with R at the beginning and 3 at the end.

"We're only three miles from Richmond," I announced.

Every few minutes after that Obie and I would argue about how far we must have gone. At last, when he thought we'd gone three and three quarters miles and I thought only a mile and a half, we saw that we were there.

We crossed a big bridge over the river, and the next step was to find a small brown house next to a stone Presbyterian church. Miss Holkum's cook had been pretty flustered when giving us the directions, and we had trouble remembering them. We must have been around to five wooden churches, or maybe to one wooden church five times, before we found a stone one with a signboard out in front of it.

"It's got to be Presbyterian," said Obie, crossing his fingers.

Joe finally got a match lit long enough for me to see a word starting with *Pr* on the signboard.

"This is it," I told them. "And if Reverend Pringle has his name hung up, that should start with those same two letters."

"You sure do read good now," said Obie respectfully, and I saw that even Joe was impressed.

Mr. Pringle didn't have his name hung up, but the house next door to the church was small and brown, so we figured it must be his. Joe thought it wasn't safe to ever wake a white man up in the middle of the night.

"It could be just enough to make him turn nasty," he warned.

We started round to the back of the house, Obie arguing that Joe was crazy and that he wasn't going to get any wetter, when we saw that Mr. Pringle wouldn't need to be woken up. There was a light in one of the downstairs windows and we could see a tall, thin, round-shouldered figure walking back and forth carrying a screaming baby. I started to squeeze through the bushes to knock on the window.

"Arthur, be quiet!" a stern voice sounded through the window. The screaming went on.

"Stop it, Arthur!"

I tapped on the window, but the sound was drowned out by the baby's yells.

"Please, Arthur?" The voice was getting desperate now, and at last Arthur took pity. The crying quieted

down and I knocked again. The tall figure was standing with his back to the window, and when he heard my tap he jumped like a startled rabbit. He put the baby down and came over to the window, opened it a little and peered through, but he couldn't see anything in the darkness.

"Reverend Pringle?" I whispered.

"Who's there?" The minister squinted nervously at us.

"There's three of us. We're going north on the underground," I told him.

"Go round to the back door and I'll let you in."

"Who are you talking to, Calvin?" asked a woman's sleepy voice from the next room.

"It's nothing, dearest. It's all right. Just go back to sleep." And to us he whispered again, "Go round to the back door."

I crawled back through the bushes and we made our way around to the door, where the Reverend Pringle let us in. He was a tall man with fuzzy yellow hair and features that didn't seem to fit together properly on his pale face. His mouth seemed to be always twitching.

"Quickly, come in. No one saw you, did they? I trust not. Goodness, you're wet through." He spoke quickly with a funny Northern accent. "We must find you something dry or you'll catch your death of cold. I wonder if I should wake Samantha. Oh, here you are, Samantha. Speaking of angels . . ." and he tittered nervously.

A fat, rather disagreeable-looking colored woman stood in the doorway holding a candle.

"What's going on here, Mr. Calvin?" she demanded suspiciously.

"Three passengers going north. We must find something dry for them. They're soaking wet."

"We're hungry, too," said Obie in a small voice.

"Of course, they're hungry, too. Can you find them something to eat, Samantha? Well, and we must think about where to put them."

"Ain't no room in this house," declared Samantha.

"You see," the minister explained to us, "ordinarily we would have been most happy to see you. But the day before yesterday my mother-in-law, who . . ." he cleared his throat, "who does not quite share my views, came to stay with us to help with the baby." Good Christian though he was, I thought he choked a little bit over that word "help."

"Bringin' with her a fancy French maid," added Samantha. "I tell you, Mr. Calvin, there ain't no room for them in this house. They got to go on."

Our hearts sank. We were about ready to drop with tiredness. There was a loud clap of thunder outside. I trembled and so did Mr. Pringle.

"No, Samantha. We can't put them out in this storm. We must rack our brains. Hmm, Mother Pennyman is in our room. We are in the living room. Arthur also. Lucy and Ellen are in the nursery. Mademoiselle what's her name is in Samantha's room. Samantha is in the laundry room. . . . Could we perhaps put the two little ones in the laundry room with you, Samantha? Just until tomorrow evening?"

"I got just about enough room to turn around as it is," snapped Samantha. "Besides, it ain't no hiding place. Mrs. Pennyman comes in there twenty times a day to make sure her things ain't being washed with the baby's diapers."

"Well, Samantha, we can just pass off the two little ones—what are your names?"

"Amos and Obadiah. And this here is Joe."

"We can just pass off Amos and Obadiah as temporary

hired help. Mother Pennyman has been urging me to do something about the weeds in the garden. And they can sleep in the corner of the laundry room with you."

Samantha didn't look very pleased, but she didn't say no.

"Now Joe," the minister went on, "presents a more difficult problem."

"Well, if you got to let them stay," grumbled Samantha, "then put him in the big closet off the living room. Nobody ever looks in there."

And so it was arranged. Samantha lit the stove and fixed us some delicious hot cakes. We had the extra clothes the Culpepper girls had given us, which weren't quite so wet as the ones we were wearing, and Mr. Pringle found some old things for Joe. Samantha washed and bandaged Obie's foot, which had a big blister, and took us off to the tiny laundry room, where we slept on a blanket on the floor. Joe went off with Mr. Pringle.

✽ 9

WE TRIED to sleep late the next day, but it wasn't easy.
First one had to get used to Arthur, who seemed to be on
a schedule of sleep one hour, scream the next, sleep
one, scream one, and so on. Then we had a whole lot of
visitors. First two tiny little girls, who we figured were
Mr. Pringle's older children, came and stared at us until
Samantha shooed them away. Then Mr. Pringle woke
us up to tell us we should sleep as late as we wanted.
He also said that we should not go outside the house,
which of course we would not have done anyhow. Next
a fierce-looking old lady woke us up with a poke of her
cane.

"What is the meaning of this?" she exclaimed.

I started to scramble to my feet, forgetting that I was
wearing only my tattered underpants, and having no
idea what to say. Luckily Samantha hurried to the rescue.

"Them's just some extra help Mr. Calvin got in, Mrs.
Pennyman," she explained.

"Help! Then what are they doing sound asleep at
eleven thirty in the morning?"

"Well, ma'am, you know how Mr. Calvin is. He don't want 'em working out in the yard while it's still so wet." Samantha was thinking fast. "And they ain't no good for nothing in the house, and they seemed awful sleepy, so he let 'em sleep."

"Sleepy!" boomed the old lady. "What you mean is lazy."

"Yes, ma'am. They is lazy, right enough. But Mr. Calvin's goin' to send 'em back again this evening, I think."

"Well, the very idea . . ." And the old lady turned and marched out.

As soon as we had got back to sleep, we were woken up again—by a scream. I opened my eyes in time to see a skirt disappearing through the doorway.

"Madame, madame, intruders in ze back room."

That would be the French maid, I figured. Mr. Pringle and Samantha soon got her calmed down again, but by now we had decided to get up.

The family had already had lunch, so Samantha gave us some leftovers and set us to clearing the table and washing the dishes. While we were clearing up we saw Mrs. Pringle, the only person of the household we hadn't met yet. She was a pretty, sickly-looking woman lying on the sofa wrapped in a shawl. I didn't think she looked very happy to see us, but I couldn't hardly blame her for that. Mr. Pringle was trying to write his sermon on the corner of the dining room table, but he kept getting up to open or close the window for his wife or to take the children away when they got too noisy.

We weren't very good at washing dishes. Samantha kept on finding bits of egg or something on the plates

I'd finished and it made her pretty mad. The mother-in-law poked her head into the kitchen and said we seemed to be very slow workers, so Obie tried to speed up. He stacked all the glasses he had dried and was just carrying them over to the cupboard when he dropped the whole stack. That brought everyone to the kitchen. Samantha and the mother-in-law scolded, Mrs. Pringle looked a little bit sicker, and Arthur screeched.

Mr. Pringle tried to be nice. He said, "Well, accidents will happen," and started to help us pick up the glass, but right away he cut his finger and Samantha sent him out of the kitchen.

After that we were put to polishing silver, sweeping the rooms and peeling potatoes. Mrs. Pennyman and her maid finally went out for a walk at about three o'clock, and we got a little break. Joe was let out of the closet long enough to have some lunch, and while he ate Mr. Pringle explained to him and me how to get to our next station in Bowling Green. I asked him how far we were from Philadelphia and he said about 245 miles. That was still an awful long way, but it was getting shorter. Mr. Strauss had told us four hundred miles just a little more than a week before.

When the mother-in-law got back from her walk they all had tea, while Mr. Pringle read aloud to them from a book of poetry. Samantha sent me in with a tray of tea things and a plate of cookies, and I hung around and passed things, because I wanted to hear what he was reading. There was a poem about a poor little girl in a shipwreck, then one that sounded very good, but I wasn't sure what it was about, and then Mr. Pringle took out a piece of paper that was stuck in the book.

"Here's something by Lowell that I cut out of a magazine," he said. It was all about slavery, and it really hit me. I still remember how it started:

> "*Men, whose boast it is that ye*
> *Come of fathers brave and free,*
> *If there breathe on earth a slave,*

Are ye truly free and brave?
If ye do not feel the chain,
When it works a brother's pain,
Are ye not base slaves indeed,
Slaves unworthy to be freed?"

Mr. Pringle read in a thin, embarrassed voice and looked around as he finished. You could see that he liked that poem, and he wanted somebody to say something. But nobody except me was even listening. Mrs. Pringle had lost a stitch in her knitting and was busy trying to find it. The mother-in-law, in a comfortable armchair, had been nodding over her sewing, and her eyes had finally closed. Mr. Pringle cleared his throat.

"Not great poetry, of course, but I must say it's very stirring."

Mrs. Pennyman raised her head with a jerk, opened her eyes, and looked around to see if anyone had noticed her napping.

"Very stirring indeed," she agreed in her booming voice. "Who did you say wrote it?"

"James Russell Lowell."

"Isn't he that abolitionist from Boston or somewhere? No, I don't care for him. I really don't care much for any of these modern poets. Don't you have any Milton or . . . That wasn't thunder again, was it?"

It wasn't thunder. It was a loud, rumbling snore from the closet. I felt sick and trembly all over. Mr. Pringle's already pale face turned a few shades paler.

"Th-th-thunder," he stuttered. "The—the—the storm must be resuming again, or . . ."

It came again. This time, maybe on purpose but more likely because his hand was shaking, Mr. Pringle dropped his teacup, and the snore was mostly covered by the clatter of breaking china.

Mrs. Pennyman looked at her son-in-law sternly.

"Well, well, this is a day for accidents," she said.

At this point Mrs. Pringle showed an unexpected presence of mind. She picked up Arthur, who was sleeping in the cradle beside her, and gave him a good pinch. The howls that followed almost drowned out the snoring. I longed to sneak over to the closet, open the door, and give Joe a pinch too, but Mrs. Pennyman's eagle eye was on me, and I didn't dare.

"Amos, get the broom," said Mr. Pringle weakly. There was a plea in his voice and in his eyes. I knew he was trying to tell me to do something, but what? I started for the kitchen door but he stopped me.

"No, no, Amos. The broom in the closet." I got the message this time.

Opening the closet door just a little, I saw Joe still sleeping soundly behind a wall of suitcases. I carefully pushed the top suitcase off the pile onto his feet. Arthur's screams covered his grunt of surprise, and I put my finger to my lips as I rummaged around. Joe blinked at me sheepishly.

"Don't seem to be no broom in here, Master Pringle," I said, closing the door again.

The broken china was soon cleared up, but it was quite a while before my heart got back to beating normally again.

We were very glad to leave the crowded little house

that night, and I'm sure everyone was glad to see us go.
Afterward, Obie did some funny imitations of Mr. Pringle
worrying, with the twitching mouth, the Northern accent
and everything, but I couldn't really laugh because I
had too much fellow feeling. I get scared awfully easily,
too, and after all I figured Mr. Pringle was a mighty
brave coward—maybe even a mighty brave man.

✺ 10

WE DIDN'T get very far that night because we were all sleepy, especially Joe. He told us that during the eighteen or so hours he'd spent in the closet, he'd only slept for those five horrible minutes. So when we got to a wooded place about six miles north of Richmond, we decided to have a nap. During the day when we rested one of us always watched while the other two slept, but that seemed silly at midnight in such a quiet spot, so we all dozed off. When I woke up a couple of hours later I had a feeling someone was close by. I sat up and strained my eyes the dark. Then I saw that it wasn't someone but something. I laughed to myself as I made out the dim shape of a raccoon munching something he was holding in his front paws. Another coon was just scurrying off into some nearby bushes. Then I got to wondering—what were they eating? I groped around for our food sack. I couldn't find it. I woke up Obie and Joe, while the raccoon, seeing my interest in him, decided to finish his meal someplace else.

We found the food sack about twenty-five feet away—

with no food in it. A few hunks of bread were spread about on the ground, and we dusted them off and put them back in the sack, but everything else was gone with the raccoons. Samantha hadn't been very generous with the food sack in the first place—I guess she thought we'd already cost the Pringles enough in broken glass and china—but we'd had enough, and now we had only a few pieces of dirty bread, with a thirty-mile hike ahead of us. And there was something else. Up to now things had seemed to be going pretty much our way, but that silly little trouble with the raccoons gave me the feeling that our luck was turning.

The next night though it really turned. We were walking along a country road north of a little place called Hanover. On the left side of the road was a wide stream, on the right a couple of small, dilapidated farmhouses. We usually tried not pass too close to houses, but this time we couldn't make a circle to the left because of the stream. A big dog chained to the porch of the first house barked furiously at us as we approached. We speeded up, hoping to get by before he had woken anyone up, but almost at once we saw a light flickering in the window. We crouched down behind some tall grass. The door of the farmhouse burst open and a bearded man carrying a shotgun stepped out. He looked around for a moment, then unchained the dog. It came bounding toward us. We jumped up from our hiding place and ran for all we were worth, back down the road we had just walked up, and then over a fence and across a field. The fence slowed the dog down a little, but soon he was behind us again. He grabbed at Joe's leg and tore a rip in his pants. Joe turned and kicked at him, and the dog backed up, growling, but when we started to run again he followed, nipping at our heels. Meanwhile the man was catching up with us.

We heard a shot fired from the road, but we all kept on running. No one had been hit.

"Towser, where are they, boy?" called the man.

The dog seemed to have been scared by the gun blast, and at the sound of his name he left us and ran back to his master. We ran on and on. The blood was pounding in my head and my throat was aching for breath. Obie was falling behind us and limping badly. I remembered his bad foot and knew that this run must be even more agonizing for him. We could hear the man and the dog still behind us. Joe took hold of Obie's arm and tried to pull him along.

"Cut over to the stream. Then we can shake 'em off," he gasped.

We turned toward our right and crossed another fence. I knew Obie couldn't keep going this way much longer, and I wondered if I could. In a few minutes we heard our pursuers clambering over the same fence. Then a shot and a yell. We all stopped and looked at each other. We were too breathless to speak, but no one seemed to have been hit. There was an awful moan some ways behind us.

"What happened?" I panted.

"Must have shot hisself," muttered Joe.

We waited, trying to catch our breaths a little and not knowing what to do next. There was another long-drawn-out moan. We started slowly to retrace our steps. When we got closer to the fence we saw a crumpled figure lying beside it. The dog was circling around his master, whimpering in an uncertain kind of way.

"Let's get out of here," whispered Joe, pulling at my sleeve.

But Obie limped closer to the man.

"You all right?" he asked. It was a silly question. Even in the darkness we could see the twisted leg and the dark, spreading stain on the trousers.

"My knee," groaned the man. "The gun went off—oh!—when I was getting over that fence. Must have hit my knee." His face was all screwed up with pain.

"Come on," muttered Joe.

"If you got a handkerchief, we could fix a bandage," suggested Obie. " 'Tain't no good to lose all that blood."

But no one had a handkerchief, and anyway the dog wouldn't have let any of us touch his master.

"Go get some help," begged the man. "I'll bleed to death here."

There was a pause. Then Obie explained: "We can't. We don't want to get caught."

"For God's sake," pleaded the man, "you got to get someone."

"Come on," whispered Joe. "We got to get out of here."

"Maybe some of your folks'll come and look for you," suggested Obie hopefully.

"No one knows I'm gone. I live by myself." There was another awful groan. It hurt just to look at him. "Go to the next house from mine. There's just an old widow lady there. She cain't do nothing to you."

We looked at each other uncertainly.

"Good night, mister," said Obie, and we climbed the fence and went on. We walked back to the road, wondering what to do. We didn't want to leave him lying there, but after all the miles we'd come and all we'd been through we just couldn't risk going for help. Joe said we were crazy to even think about it. We passed the first house. The door was wide open and the chain was hanging from the porch. We still hadn't made up our minds. We reached the second house.

"I'll go tell her," said Obie.

"Come on," urged Joe, grabbing him by the arm. "You'll get us all catched."

"They'll find him in the morning. Anyhow, I don't guess he was hurt that bad," I said, trying to convince myself and Obie both. "I guess he was putting on some."

We went on up the road, maybe a hundred yards, nobody saying anything.

Many times along the way I'd thought about how, when it was all over, I'd tell Pa, and later on Mama too, about all the things that had happened to us, and I'd imagined how they'd look proud and say we'd done real well. Now I thought about that again. "I'll have to skip this part," I told myself. "They wouldn't want to know we'd let someone bleed to death." I turned around quickly.

"You go on," I said. "I'll catch up with you."

I ran back to the farmhouse, knocked at the door, and waited for the widow. The door opened and my heart sank. There stood a hefty young man well over six feet tall. He looked at me narrowly.

"What you want?"

"Please, sir, your neighbor there, he's hurt real bad. He's in a field over thataway."

I turned and jumped down the porch steps and tried to run. I tripped over something in the darkness and fell flat on my face. Before I could scramble up I felt an ironlike grip on my arm. I was hauled inside. A bunch of people was standing around in night clothes, rubbing their eyes. There did even seem to be a widow, but what hadn't been explained was that she lived with two grown sons and a half-grown daughter.

"This nigger says Jud's hurt over in some field," said the man who was holding me. "Must have been that commotion we heard a while back. We better go check."

"Bring the kid along. He can show us where."

"He'll try to get away. Got a rope, Ma?"

The widow looked around while her sons pulled pants on over their nightshirts.

"Cain't find no rope," she said after a while. "Use the clothesline."

Someone went to get it, and they tied my hands behind my back. By some kind of lucky instinct—I'm sure I wasn't thinking at that point—I held my hands thumb to thumb while they were being tied. The men told their sister to come along and keep an eye on me, and we all set off. I led the way in a kind of daze, feeling just like a trapped animal. Nobody said much. Finally we got to the wounded man and the dog.

"Thank God you've come," he groaned. "Thank God, thank God."

He could have thanked me too, but he didn't.

They looked him over and saw that they'd have to carry him back. There was a lot of talk, but I wasn't listening. I just remember one thing.

The girl asked who I was, and Jud—that was what they called him—said: "Some runaway, I reckon. Hang on to him."

I looked at him then, but he turned away his face.

Going back, my legs suddenly felt so heavy I could hardly move them. I kept on stumbling and falling behind the others.

"Get a move on him," called one of the men. The girl yanked at the rope, and it spun me half around. I felt as if my arms were being pulled out of the shoulders. I felt as if I was going to be sick, and thought, not now, not in front of them.

Somehow we all got back to the first farmhouse, and the men carried Jud inside. Then they got the dog back on his chain and took me out to a tool shed back of the house. They threw me in and padlocked the door. As they walked away they were talking about which one would go get the doctor and which would ride down to Hanover to tell Jud's brother.

Now at last I was alone. I sank down on the dirt floor and pressed my face against the ground. I wanted to cry—maybe it would help me not to think—but no tears came. All those miles, all those dangers, and it had ended like this! I would be sent back to the Brickers. Master Bricker would question me: Why had I run away? How could I be so ungrateful? I'd get beaten and probably sold to some stranger. Maybe Obie would make it though. Maybe Obie . . .

"Amos."

I sat up. That was Obie's voice.

"Amos." The whisper came through a crack in the boards.

"Obie, is that you?" I hardly dared believe it.

"Yes. Listen. It'll be light in an hour or two. We got to get you out of there. You tied up?"

I put my hands back to back and twisted and wiggled them.

"Not now I ain't," I answered.

"Feel around and see if there's any boards loose," he whispered. "The door's padlocked and I cain't do nothing with it."

I felt around. No loose boards.

"You got a shovel in there? Maybe we could dig you out."

I felt around again. There was a shovel and we both went to work. The ground was hard as stone, and after about twenty minutes we'd made a hole only about big enough for my hand to pass through. We'd never make it before daylight.

"You go on, Obie. If you hang around, they'll just catch you too." I felt as if something was breaking inside of me as I said it.

"Amos, quick, find a screwdriver or something like that, and pass it out to me."

I knew by the excitement in his voice that he had a real idea this time. I found a screwdriver and shoved it through the hole to him. Next thing I heard him working away on the door. He was taking off the hinges! It was only about ten minutes later that the door swung open from the wrong side, and I was free again.

As we crept out and around the side of the house the dog started to bark again. We ran. I heard the door open and I looked back. There was Jud. He had pulled himself out to the porch and again he had his gun. But he didn't shoot and he didn't unchain the dog.

"Get out of here, you dirty, lousy, no-good niggers," he yelled. "Get out of here."

His voice was full of hatred, but I wasn't sure if it was for us or for himself.

❧ 11

As soon as I'd got myself a little bit collected again I asked Obie where Joe was.

"I guess he's up ahead someplace," he answered.

"How'd you lose him?"

"He came back with me to see what had happened to you, and we hung around awhile, but when we saw you on that rope with all those people he just thought you were a goner for sure."

I nodded. "I just thought so, too."

"Well, he went on up the road a piece, and he hauled me along with him. He said he wasn't going to let them get me too. He was going to take me all the way to Pa hisself."

"How'd you get away from him then?" I asked.

"Bit him again."

"Well, most likely we'll catch him up in Bowling Green. He knew how to find our station there." But inside I wondered if we'd ever make it to Bowling Green ourselves.

We were dog-tired and we were hungry—we'd hardly

eaten for more than twenty-four hours. Obie's foot hurt with every step, and by now my feet were getting pretty blistered up, too. Most of all, though, we were scared. It was getting light already, and we knew that soon the word would spread that escaping slaves were in the neighborhood and everybody would be looking for us. Maybe they'd put dogs on our trail. We had to get to Bowling Green, to at least a little bit of safety, as quick as we could, but we figured we were still almost twenty miles away.

We started by swimming the stream that ran along beside the road. That would put the dogs off our track, and we did it several times during the morning. It was just a small stream, but every time we swam it I was afraid Obie wouldn't have the strength to make it across. The last time I had to pull him most of the way. He didn't grumble much though, and said the cold water made his foot feel better.

We kept going the whole day, most of the time on our stomachs, crawling through high grass or in ditches. When we got to wooded places we would run from tree to tree, always looking around before we moved. Twice we saw groups of men who seemed to be hunting and we wondered if they were hunting for us. They didn't see us though.

Then about five o'clock in the evening we were crawling along in a ditch beside the road, longing for the sun to set and the darkness to hide us again, when we saw a small group coming along the road behind us. We flattened ourselves in the ditch and waited. Even before I could see who they were I felt that there was something

terrible about them. Then as they came closer I peeked
through the tall grass and saw. There were three white
men, one gray-haired, the other two younger. The young
men both carried guns. In the middle was Joe. Blood was
trickling down his face from a cut on his forehead, and
there was a look of awful terror in his eyes. After they
passed we followed along behind them, staying out of
sight in the ditch, hoping we could help and knowing
that we couldn't. A couple of times they passed houses

on the other side of the road and the people came out
to gawk at Joe and ask the white men how they'd caught
him. A group of boys with fishing poles stopped to laugh
and jeer, and later a woman passed, going in the other
direction, with a goat and a little girl. The girl ran over
to see what was happening, but her mother called her
back, and as they went by I heard her scolding, "Don't
stare, honey. It ain't polite. He got troubles enough as
'tis." Then they walked away.

I looked at Obie and saw that his lips were moving.
"Please, God, please, let Joe get free."

The prayer wasn't answered—at least not the way we
hoped. We followed the little group till they came to a
place where there was a wood on the other side of the
road. Joe was staggering as the others pulled him along,
half dragging, half supporting him. Suddenly, without
any warning, he wrenched himself free and bolted into
the woods. There was a lot of shouting and some shots.
The two young men rushed after Joe. We waited, sick
with horror. After a while, the two young men came out
of the wood carrying Joe by his arms and legs. They laid
him down on the road, and the old man knelt down and
put his ear to Joe's chest. He listened for a little, then
stood up and said angrily:

"What'd you do that for? D'you think his master's going to pay us anything for a carcass?"

I turned my head away. I felt sick and dizzy and I
didn't want to see any more. I wanted to hate all the
white folks, all of them, and suddenly I felt angry at the
ones who had been good to us because they wouldn't let
me hate them.

The white men carried Joe's body away, and we went on, too. We had to stop more and more often now, one of us always watching while the other slept. We finally got to Bowling Green sometime after midnight, I guess. On our way into town we passed a couple of men on horseback. We figured it must be a patrol, and we flattened ourselves against a wall. They rode on past us.

Our station in Bowling Green was the Johnson house. The Johnsons were free Negroes and they lived on the outskirts of town in the Negro section. The streets weren't marked, and the houses all looked pretty much the same, all small and rundown. However, we finally found a house that looked a little better than the others, with a small garden in front and a sign, MARY JOHNSON, EXPERT DRESSMAKING. We knocked at the back door. A woman with a lamp opened it. When she saw us she didn't ask any questions. She just pulled us inside and closed the door. Then she turned to her husband, who was just coming into the kitchen, rubbing his eyes sleepily.

"Here's two passengers, Jack," she said.

Mr. Johnson was a big, handsome man with a friendly, pleasant way about him. Mrs. Johnson wasn't such an easy-looking person, but you could see right away that she was an arranger, and that was what we needed. Before she even gave us anything to eat she showed us our hiding place. A couple of boards in the floor could be moved and the earth had been dug away beneath.

"We heard about you fellows already," Mr. Johnson told us. "There was a deputy here this afternoon looking for you. But we thought there was three."

"There was." I was too weary to start telling about Joe, and they didn't press us.

"How'd the deputy know to come here?" Obie asked, sounding pretty nervous.

Mr. Johnson laughed. "One of our good neighbors must have noticed that we get a lot of company. This deputy, he said you shot a white man down near Hanover. Said you wounded him pretty bad."

We just shook our heads. Again we were too tired to explain.

Mrs. Johnson set some hoecake and stewed apples on the kitchen table and told us to sit down. My stomach, my whole body, even my whole soul had been aching and aching for food for two days already, but now somehow I didn't even want to look at it. I pushed myself to eat the apples and looked over across the table at Obie. He was just sitting there with tears streaming down his face.

"Don't cry now, Obie," I told him. "It's over now."

He didn't answer. He just laid his head down on the table and his shoulders shook with sobs.

"It's over now," I told him again.

The Johnsons looked at each other and at me. We all wanted to comfort him, but what was there to say? But Obie was so tired he couldn't even cry for long. Soon he was just sitting there, gasping for breath. Mr. Johnson coaxed him to eat a little and washed and bandaged his foot. Then Mrs. Johnson lifted up the floor boards and we crawled into the hiding place. I was just so wound up, though, I couldn't go to sleep right away, and as I lay there I heard the Johnsons talking.

"How're we going to get those children out of here, honey?" asked Mr. Johnson. "They're combing the roads for them, and they sure ain't safe in this house."

"I got to think, Jack. You go back to sleep. I'll figure a plan." And the way she said it I was pretty sure she would.

The next thing I remember, Mrs. Johnson was shaking me awake. I felt stiff and achy all over.

"Get up and have some breakfast," she said.

I crawled out from our hiding place, still feeling light-headed from lack of sleep and food, and took the steaming bowl she handed me. Six or seven Johnson children stood around the kitchen, staring at us with big solemn eyes.

Mrs. Johnson asked, "Think you can keep going one more day?"

It sounded more like an order than a question and we nodded wearily.

"First thing, then, is to get you out of this town. We got a plan for that. Then my husband's going to hide you in the woods where he works. After the other men go home, he'll pretend he forgot something and go back. He'll take you as far as the cattle track that leads to the Webbers' farm. It's sixteen miles, but it's an easy way and you can make it in one night, and when you get there you can rest up for a while. They're good people and they'll take care of you."

Mr. Johnson turned to Obie. "You'll come up to the woods with me. That's my job, chopping trees. Lots of the men bring their boys, so that won't cause any trouble, and, Johnny," he added, turning to his eldest son, "that means you stay home today."

Mrs. Johnson picked up a skirt and handed it to me.

"This here's for you. You're going to be a girl for today. They're going to forget their lunch, and about ten minutes after they're gone, you're going to be running up that road carrying a bag of food, and if anyone asks you, you're taking lunch to Daddy."

"Seems like my big day for forgetting," laughed Mr. Johnson.

I ran my hand over my close-cropped head. What was I supposed to do for hair?

Mrs. Johnson chuckled and held up a red polkadot bandanna. "Don't worry," she said. "You may not look beautiful, but you'll look like a girl."

"We got to get going," said Mr. Johnson. "If I got to hide these fellows I want to be the first man out in the forest."

He look up his ax and his lunch.

"Oh, I forgot. I got to forget this," he said, putting down his lunch again. And he and Obie set off.

Mrs. Johnson fixed me up in the skirt and bandanna—she even put a jingly bracelet on my arm—while the children watched wide-eyed. Then she took me to the road that led out of town, wished me good luck, and went home.

A little way up the road I saw a white man with a bristly black beard sitting on a horse. He seemed to be watching the road. I wanted to turn around and run back, but I knew by now that boldness was the safest thing, so I went straight up to him.

" 'Scuse me, sir, Did you see my papa and my little brother go by this way?"

"Let's see now. There was a man and a little boy went

by. A woodcutter." His voice was pleasanter than his face.

"Is they very far ahead? Papa left his lunch home, and I got to catch him up."

"Well, I'd say they passed ten minutes ago. You can catch them if you get a move on."

So I got a move on. I ran as fast as my aching feet would carry me, and pretty soon I saw them ahead of me on the road. Then I slowed down, keeping them in sight, but making sure not to catch up with them.

After about three miles they turned off the road and I hurried up. I passed one woodcutter already hacking away at a tree, but he didn't even look around at me. It wasn't hard to find Mr. Johnson because he was singing at the top of his lungs. I followed the sound and there he was in a clearing, just getting ready to swing the ax. But Obie was nowhere in sight. Mr. Johnson read my anxious face and laughed.

"Want to play hide and seek?" he suggested. "Your brother's right close here."

I searched around a bit just to be polite, though I didn't feel like playing games. There was an old abandoned cart with a broken axle and a missing wheel at the other side of the clearing. As I got near it Mr. Johnson said, "Warmer, warmer." I looked all around it and then inside. It was full of dead leaves. Then I heard a giggle down under the leaves.

"All right, you found him," said Mr. Johnson. "Now get in yourself and I'll cover you both up."

In just a few minutes I was dozing off, lulled by the

rhythmical beat of the ax. I was woken up sometime later by the sound of voices, Mr. Johnson's and a new voice.

"Say, Jack, there was a deputy just out here looking for a couple of runaway slave boys. Says they may be dangerous."

"Goodness, boss, what kind of dangerous?"

"Well, I don't exactly know. He said something about some farmer down near Hanover getting hurt pretty bad. Anyway, there's a reward for them."

"Do they think they're around here, boss?"

"Well, they could be. They're probably headed north."

There was a pause, then the new voice went on, sounding kind of apologetic, "Well, you know I don't really go for that kind of thing, slave catching. You know I'm kind of a softie, but, heck, somebody's going to collect that reward, so why not me?"

"Why not, boss?"

"Well, and if you're the first one to spot them, I'll cut you in on it, Jack. So keep your eyes open. The road's pretty well watched, so they might just try to slip through these woods."

"O. K., boss. I'll keep my eyes open. Sure could use a little bonus." He laughed in his carefree, jolly way, and the boss went off, never suspecting that the laugh was on him.

After the men had all gone home that evening and the woods were quiet again, Mr. Johnson came back and shook us out of the leaves. He'd saved us some of his lunch, and after we'd eaten, he lead us through the woods about four miles. He carried Obie most of the way to spare his bad foot. When we reached the end of the wood, he left us.

"It's about thirteen miles now to Webber's farm. Just follow this here track, and you'll be there in time for breakfast tomorrow morning." And he went off through the dark woods, whistling.

We walked on and off all night. Obie leaned on my shoulder so as not to put too much weight on his foot, but I didn't feel like a very steady crutch myself. I guess I still hadn't caught up on sleep and food, and a couple of times I was afraid I was going to faint. Between us we had to take a lot of rests that night, and when the sun rose we still hadn't reached the Webber farm. We knew it couldn't be much farther, though, and our cattle track seemed to be pretty deserted, so we decided to keep going.

The country we were walking through was turning green in the early morning sun, with wavy grass and dark clumps of trees. Usually that kind of country makes me feel good all through, but now it didn't seem right anymore. It seemed like a cheat. I still had Joe too much on my mind, and I couldn't stop thinking about him— not just how he'd died, but how he'd lived. The world had taken everything he wanted away from him and given him nothing back, and now how could it look so green and kind and open again?

It must have been seven or eight in the morning when we finally saw the big white barn and long low chicken house that we were looking for. A couple of dogs, a shaggy sheep dog and a fat little fox terrier, came toward us, barking their heads off but wagging their tails at the same time. I remember thinking right away as I watched those wagging tails that they must belong to friendly people.

A tall, lanky, towheaded boy came out of the barn to scold the dogs. "Shep, Pixie, where's your manners?" he said. He studied us for a moment, then took the piece of grass he was sucking out of his mouth.

"Looking for something?" he asked.

"We're looking for the Webber farm."

"Well, you found it. I'm Will Webber. Come on with me."

❦12

WE SLEPT all that day in the Webbers' hayloft. It was the first time we'd felt more or less safe for a week or so.

In the evening the tall boy we'd seen in the morning came and told us to come and wash and have supper. A couple of his younger brothers came with him, both towheads with friendly, mischievous faces.

"I'm Ben," announced the younger one.

"I'm Ned," said his brother. "What's your names?"

We introduced ourselves.

"Amos—but that's a boy's name," said Ned.

"How come thee's got a boy's name?" chimed in Ben.

I looked at them in confusion for a minute, and then I looked at my clothes. I'd completely forgotten that I was still wearing a skirt. I felt my cheeks getting hot and my ears tingling as I pulled off the bandanna and stepped out of the skirt.

Both the younger boys doubled up with laughter, and Obie joined in.

"Put that stuff on again. Thee can fool Alice."

"Thee can fool Mother and Dad. Put it on again."

Will, the oldest, was grinning too, but when he saw my embarrassment he told the others to stop pestering me.

"That was a mighty clever disguise," he added, and right away I felt that I'd like to be friends with him.

They took us into the farmhouse. It was a comfortable-looking old house, rather untidy with books and toys lying around, and a delicious smell was coming from the kitchen.

I was still feeling kind of ruffled over being taken for a girl, but when I saw that we were supposed to eat with the family I really got worried, because we'd never eaten with white folks before, and I didn't know how to act. At home we didn't have any special table manners—we hardly could because we didn't have a table.

The whole family was gathered around in the dining room. Mr. Webber was tall and thin and thoughtful looking, like Will. Mrs. Webber had a rather plain round face and a lively manner like the younger children. There was a daughter, too, called Alice, who came in between Ned and Ben, and two more younger boys.

Everyone told us their names, and we told them ours, and we all sat down. "Oh, well," I thought, "I'll just watch what they do. I just hope Obie has sense enough to do the same." But Obie didn't. He started off by drinking his whole glass of milk while Mr. Webber was getting set to say grace. The children giggled and the parents smiled, but I didn't think it was funny at all. I tried to kick Obie under the table, but I got Alice instead.

She said, "Ouch. What's that?" but no one paid any attention.

Mrs. Webber gave us chicken and mashed potatoes. Obie ate the chicken with his hands and the potatoes and vegetables with a spoon. Spoons were all we had to eat with at home, but I saw that even Ben, who looked to be only about six years old, was using a fork. Then Obie made things even worse. He isn't really so boastful, but sometimes he sounds that way. That evening, what with the long sleep and the safety and the chicken, he was in a really fine mood. He started telling the Webbers all our adventures, talking with his mouth full, and making us sound an awful lot braver than we really were. When he got to the part about me getting locked in the toolshed, he really laid it on. I wanted to give him a good hard kick, but I didn't dare try again. Obie was still talking away when Ben slowly pushed back his chair, went over to his mother and whispered in her ear. I could see that it was something about us, and I just wanted to run away and hide. Even Obie paused for a moment.

Then Mrs. Webber smiled at us. "Ben thinks you boys are real heroes," she said. "He wants to sleep in the hay-loft with you tonight."

"Oh, Mother, Ben's too little. Couldn't I? Please?"

Ned and Ben both started pleading with their mother for the honor of sleeping in the loft with us, and while they argued, I stopped worrying about how to hold my knife and fork and noticed for the first time how good the chicken tasted.

We spent two weeks at the Webbers', resting up and waiting for Obie's foot to get all healed up. Ned and Ben took turns sleeping in the loft with us, and we helped them with their chores so they would have more time to play with us—or rather with Obie, because he was much more for playing than me. The three of them spent hours climbing up and sliding down the rope that hung from the barn rafters, or just wrestling and throwing hay at each other. I mostly just watched. Sometimes Will would come and watch, too, with a shy smile and usually a book in his hand, and his terrier, Pixie, at his

heels. I could see that he wanted to be friendly but
didn't know quite how to start. One day I asked him
if he would help me learn to read, and after that we
spent a lot of time together. He'd start out with a reading
lesson, and after a while we'd get to talking about something. He was the first person outside my own family
that I really liked talking to.

One time I asked him something I'd wondered about
ever since we'd stayed with Mr. McNaul, why the
Quakers said "thee" instead of "you." (The Webbers
were Quakers, too, and Obie was always trying to imitate
their way of speaking, but he never seemed to get it
quite right and would say "thee" when he meant the
whole family and "you" when he was talking to one of
the boys.) The way Will explained it, people used to
say "you" to anyone above them, a duke or a king, or
maybe just a rich person, and "thee" to just ordinary
folks, but the Quakers thought you should show the
same amount of respect for everyone. "Thee" had always sounded kind of silly to me before, but after he
explained that to me I liked it. But Will said he only used
"thee" in the family or when his parents were around.
He felt too embarrassed to talk that way in school or in
town.

"The funny part is," he added, "I agree with all the
things Quakers believe, but I still sort of wish I was
something else, something more ordinary. Just like thee
probably sometimes wishes thee were white."

"No, I don't," I answered honestly, "but then black
always seemed more ordinary to me."

That seemed to tickle Will. "Well, I reckon it would,"

he said. "Where my mother was raised in Philadelphia, the Quakers are thick as flies, but here in Virginia you feel like kind of a freak, kind of different."

"But anyhow, different isn't always worse. It could be better."

"That's just exactly what Dad says. And he says it's only when you're sort of a middle-aged boy, about my age, that you really mind so much being different. He says when you're younger, below ten or so, you don't hardly notice, and after twenty you're proud of it." Then after a pause he added, "I don't know whether he's right, though, 'cause a lot of grown-ups seem to like to be usual, just like me."

"Well, maybe they kind of stopped growing up before they ever hit twenty. Maybe . . ." As usual I didn't know how to say what I meant. I was all wound up in the words when Ned came running into the barn and changed the subject.

"Hey, Amos," he announced in a very important voice. "Guess what Mother and Dad are doing. They're planning the next part of your trip."

"Let's go help them," suggested Will.

Mr. and Mrs. Webber were sitting at the dining room table as we came in. He looked glum and she looked mad. She was telling him, in the same voice she used for scolding the children, that she was not going to allow us to go any farther on foot. Mr. Webber told her there was no other way, that there were more underground stations in the border states, and that we'd have much more help from now on. Mrs. Webber set her jaw and said she didn't care. We were not going to walk another two hundred miles, we were not going to walk another two miles, and that was that.

"I got an idea, Dad," said Will hesitantly. "Grandfather's always asking for one of us to go up to Philadelphia and visit him. Why couldn't I go by train, and take Amos and Obie with me?"

"How could thee take them with thee?"

"They could pretend to be servants."

Mr. Webber smiled a patient, long-suffering smile.

"Will, those railroads are watched. A Quaker farm boy traveling with two Negro valets would have every slave catcher in the state following him."

"I guess so. I wish I could just stuff them in my luggage."

"Please go outside, boys. Your mother and I are . . ."

"Wait. That's it," Mrs. Webber almost shouted. "Send them to Philadelphia in Will's luggage."

"My dear, we must be practical; we must be realistic . . ." protested Mr. Webber.

But his wife was no longer listening. She had jumped up from her chair and bustled out of the room and was fairly flying up the two flights of stairs to the attic. Will, Ned and I clattered up the steps behind her, and Mr. Webber brought up the rear, still muttering about practicality and realism.

There were three trunks in the attic. Mrs. Webber looked them over critically.

"Ned, run and find Obie," she ordered as she pulled open the lid of the biggest trunk. "Amos, get in and see if thee can fit."

I climbed into the musty-smelling trunk and curled

up. Will was inspecting another trunk, smaller but with
a curved lid.

"This one would be better," he said. "It couldn't be
put upside down."

I got out of the big trunk and into the smaller one, where I was soon joined by an excited Obie. It was too tight a squeeze. They couldn't close the lid on us.

"Besides," said Mrs. Webber, "there's got to be a little extra space for padding. Try the big one again."

We did. There was just enough room for Obie and me to sit side by side, with our knees pulled up under our chins and our heads bent forward.

"What are we supposed to breathe?" said Obie doubtfully. "I mean, after a while we might run out of air in here."

"Hmm . . ." Mr. Webber studied the trunk. "I could bore a row of air holes on each side here, under the handle straps."

So it seemed that the idea was practical and realistic after all.

❧ 13

THE EXCITEMENT of the next few days was like the excitement before we first left home, only this time we didn't have to keep it to ourselves. It was shared all around.

Mrs. Webber wrote to her father in Philadelphia. Mr. Webber took the big trunk down from the attic to the barn and set to work making improvements on it. Obie and I and the Webber boys tried to help, and made suggestions, and generally got in the way.

First he made three air holes on each side under the leather straps which served as handles. No one would ever notice them from the outside. Then he put a false, rounded top on the trunk, so that we wouldn't have to worry about being turned upside down. The other chestlike trunk had given him the idea. He cut three sections off the rim of an old wagon wheel and screwed them to the lid of the trunk. Then he stretched a piece of canvas over the sections of wheel and stuffed straw in the hollow places between the false top and the real one, and last of all we painted the whole trunk so that the canvas piece matched up with the rest.

The day after we painted the trunk the letter arrived from Philadelphia. Will would be more than welcome to come for a visit. His grandfather would meet him at the station and he could bring all the luggage he wanted, "including those two black cases." I saw that even white people had to pretty careful about what they said in letters.

That letter arrived on a Friday and we set out the following Monday, because the Webbers didn't approve of traveling on Sunday, or First Day, as they called it. I especially remember that last Saturday night at the Webbers', because we woke up in the middle of the night and found that Will's fox terrier, Pixie, had had five puppies. They were cute, tiny little things, black and white and brown, and Pixie lay there looking so proud and satisfied. Will and Ned and Obie and I stood around and admired them, and, feeling inside myself, I realized that the awful hurt of Joe's death was starting to heal. Not that I'd forgotten it; I guess I never will.

On Monday morning, August 8th, we got up before sunrise. The whole family crowded around to wish us Godspeed, and Mrs. Webber kissed us just as though we'd been her own children. Will, looking nervous and uncomfortable in his best clothes, sat beside his father in the buggy. We climbed into the trunk and scrunched up, and the lid closed over our heads. Mr. Webber shouted to the horses, and off we went.

At first the folded-up feeling of being inside the trunk was quite exciting, but already by the time we got to Fredericksburg, where we were to catch the stagecoach, we were aching all over and wondering how we could stand a whole day of it. Luckily we were about half an hour early for the coach, so Mr. Webber drove out of town to a quiet place and let us have a good stretch. Then we went back to the coach stop.

When the stagecoach finally rolled up, Mr. Webber helped the driver load us aboard. I heard him explain that the trunk must be handled with the utmost care because his wife had packed some presents for her father inside—breakable and of great sentimental value, he added.

Then followed the ten most uncomfortable hours of my life. I felt as if I would never be able to straighten myself out again, but even in my pain I remembered that every jolt and bounce was bringing us nearer to freedom.

Finally we arrived in Washington. Will took a room for the night in the coach inn, and he and the driver carried us carefully upstairs. Then he locked the door and unlocked the trunk. He was very much relieved to see us still there and still alive, and we were even more relieved to get out. We staggered over to the double bed and lay there for a couple of hours. Will offered us some food, but all we wanted was fruit. We could almost feel our muscles slowly uncurling. When it got dark Will got into his nightshirt, said his prayers, and stretched out beside us on the bed.

"Tomorrow at this time," he whispered, "you'll be on free soil."

"Day after tomorrow, we'll be with Pa," said Obie.

"Sh!"

There were footsteps and voices in the hall outside

our door. There was a knock. Without a word Obie and I rolled out of and under the bed. Hiding was starting to come naturally. Will wasn't used to this kind of excitement, though, and I knew he was scared. After a second knock, he asked in a voice all squeaky with nervousness, "Who's there?"

"Open the door, will you, son. We're all full up, and we got another gentleman wanting a room. We're going to have to put him in with you."

"Sorry, mister, but this room . . ."

Will opened the door to argue, and that was a mistake right there. While he stood pleading with the landlord, the other gentleman bustled in, put down his suitcase, and started to pull off his boots.

"It isn't fair, mister. Please. It's only a single room." There was a note of desperation in Will's voice.

"A single room, perhaps, but a double bed. Relax, my boy. Mr. Stout here won't eat you, and I might give you a slight rebate on your bill. I trust you'll pass a comfortable night, Mr. Stout. Good night."

"But, sir, I don't want a rebate. I just want to be alone. Please . . ."

The door slammed shut in the middle of Will's speech and he sank back onto the bed. In the corner of the room Mr. Stout had got his socks off, and now he was removing his vest, shirt and undershirt. His figure, at least the lower half of it, which was all we could see, seemed to fit his name.

Under the bed Obie and I were in trouble. The dust of several years seemed to be collected there, tickling our noses every time we breathed.

Obie exploded: *"Ah choo!"*

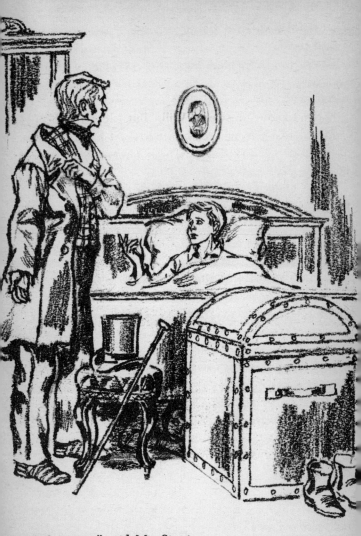

"Bless you," said Mr. Stout.

"I feel sick," said Will. He sounded sick, too.

I also felt a sneeze coming on and grabbed my nose.

That awful dust! Then it came.

"*Ah choo!*"

"Bless you," repeated Mr. Stout, pausing as he unpacked his nightshirt. "I hope you're not coming down with a cold, my boy. You don't have a fever, do you?"

"I don't know," answered Will. "But I feel awful."

Mr. Stout went over to the bed to get a closer look at Will. "Oh, Lord, don't make us sneeze again right now," I prayed.

"Why, boy, you're shivering like a leaf. And it's eighty-five degrees in the moonlight. I believe you do have a fever."

He hurried over to the corner of the room and started putting on his clothes again.

"I believe I'll just see if the landlord can't find me another room. Nothing personal, boy. You're a fine-looking, well-mannered lad, but I'm going to Richmond on a business trip, and I just can't afford to get sick."

He was getting his boots on again now.

"Anything I can get you, boy? You look to me like you got a fever."

"No, thank you, sir. I feel like I just need to be alone," said Will through chattering teeth.

Mr. Stout took his suitcase and went out. Obie and I waited for a while to see if he'd come back, but he didn't, so we joined Will on top of the bed again.

"One thing, Will," said Obie in his most superior-sounding voice, "if anything like this happens again, try not to sound so rattled."

Will was mad. "If it weren't for my lucky shivers," he snapped back, "thee'd still be sneezing away under the bed. And just one more remark like that and thee may be again."

The next day was so easy it almost didn't seem natural. The only really hard part was folding up our stiff, sore limbs and packing them into the trunk again. Then Will and the landlord carried us downstairs.

"How are you feeling today?" asked the landlord.

I wished I could have kicked Will when he answered, "Fine."

"Well, you sure had that poor Mr. Stout concerned about you last night," said the landlord reproachfully. "As a matter of fact he went over to the hotel across the way."

Will found a cab outside, and we rattled over the city streets for about half an hour. Then came the noisy confusion of the railroad station. We were almost glad to be in the trunk as we heard Will asking questions in a more and more flustered voice.

"Please, mister, where do they sell tickets?" "Please, can I get a ticket to Philadelphia here?" "Where could I find the train for Philadelphia, mister?" and on and on. Then came an unexpected question.

"Mister, would I be allowed to ride in the luggage car with my trunk?"

We pricked up our ears for the answer.

"Don't make no difference to me where you ride, sonny, just as long as you pay your fare."

A moment later we were heaved up and plonked down. We figured we were in the luggage car. Then there was a long wait. After a while the handle strap on my side was pulled out and Will started whispering through the air holes.

"I'm going to ride in here, too. I'll open the lid as soon as . . ."

"Who are you talking to there, sonny? There's no live-stock in that there trunk, is there?" It was the same gruff voice that had given Will permission to ride in the luggage car.

"No, sir. I was . . . I was just . . . I guess I was talking to myself."

Luckily, the conductor, or whoever he was, was too busy to be suspicious, and he soon went away again, but Will didn't try any more conversation.

At last the train started to move, at first slowly and jerkily. Will opened the lid of the trunk and we sat up. Now we could feel the wheels going faster and faster, faster than we'd ever moved in our lives. Will sat beside the trunk, ready to close the lid when the train slowed down or pulled into a station. Sometimes he looked out through a crack where the door didn't quite close and tried to figure out where we were. We stopped in one very big city—must be Baltimore, Will said—and then passed a river—Will thought it was the Susquehanna. He was pretty good on geography.

"Is it still slave country, or free?" Obie kept on asking.

"Well, I guess it's still slave. I guess we're still in Maryland."

But the last time Obie asked, Will squinted through the crack for a long time, studying the landscape as if that would give him the answer. Then he said:

"Well, I reckon we're in Pennsylvania now. That's a free state."

What happened then happened inside of us, and it wouldn't be any use to try to explain.

Will's grandfather met us in Philadelphia and took us home, still in the trunk. He gave us a great welcome and a good supper, but my stomach felt so queasy I could hardly eat. It was like that last breakfast in the cabin.

We asked him how far it was to Lemhorn, and he said a little under twenty miles. Obie wanted to start right out.

"Good gracious, child, what can thee be thinking about? It's dark already," said the old gentleman, laughing.

Obie shrugged. "We've walked hundreds of miles in the dark," he said. "We like to walk in the dark." I could just see that it was going to take a few weeks before Obie would be fit to live with again.

"And you've still got to be careful," Will reminded us. "With this Fugitive Slave Law they've got now . . ."

His grandfather looked grave and nodded, but we weren't worried about the Fugitive Slave Law. We'd never even heard of it. For us Pennsylvania was the Promised Land.

"In any case," said the old gentleman, "I want to de-

liver you to your father in style. You three go to bed
now, and I'll pop over to a banker friend of mine. He's
an ardent abolitionist, and I know he'll lend Amos and
Obadiah his second carriage for an occasion like this."

Sure enough the next morning a carriage, with a
coachman in a fancy uniform, drove up to the house.
Obie and I were ready—we'd been ready for hours—
when it arrived. What was hard then was saying good-by
to Will. We promised to write to each other as soon as
I learned to write.

"Thee should have a last name, though," he said, fishing out an address book from his pocket.

"I do. Carpenter. Amos Carpenter." I thought it
sounded pretty good. I didn't know our address, but the
grandfather said that Lemhorn was such a small place
we probably wouldn't need one.

"I hate writing letters, though," said Will, kicking at
the carriage wheel. "It's not the same as talking." And
I knew what he meant.

Our driver was very cheerful and friendly, and told us
a lot of jokes, but he didn't go very fast. A little way
out of town he met a friend of his and they had a long
gossip while we fidgeted in the carriage. Then he com-
plained that his throat was dry from so much talking
and he stopped at a tavern to wet it. He came back
friendlier than ever, but it was almost time for lunch,
and after lunch he had to have a snooze. Then he drove
steadily for a while, but by midafternoon he needed
some more refreshment.

"I won't be long, lads," he promised as he pulled up in
front of another tavern.

Obie and I looked at each other desperately, and then at a signpost on the road ahead. LEMHORN, 6 MILES, it said.

"Take your time," I told him. "We can walk from here."

There was a bit of an argument, but not much. Obie wanted to walk, too, and the driver didn't especially want to drive.

"Good luck, lads," he called after us. "I'll be drinking your health."

The warm summer sun shone down on us, and the road felt hot and good beneath our feet. It seemed right somehow to be walking the last few miles of our journey.

When we got to Lemhorn, the sun was already getting lower in the sky. It was just a little bitsy place, smaller than Searsville. We asked the first person we met, a well-dressed lady, where we could find Henry Carpenter.

"Never heard of Henry Carpenter," she replied and swept by.

A man was digging in his garden nearby, so we asked him.

"You mean that colored fellow, don't you?"

"Yes, sir."

"The one with the funny teeth or the other one?"

"The other one," I said. At least I couldn't remember anything funny about Pa's teeth.

"Well, I'm not sure where he lives. But I know he gets his food at the general store down the other side of the street. The storekeeper could probably tell you where he lives."

We went down the other side of the street to the store. There were several women in there, and they all looked

curiously at us while we waited our turn. Finally we got
a chance to ask the storekeeper, and he did know where
Pa lived.

"Turn right at the next corner, then left on the dirt
road. He's fixed himself up a little hut out there, a few
hundred feet down the dirt road."

We followed his directions in a kind of daze of excitement. All of a sudden I wished we were a little farther away, or else already there. I felt shy, and I let
Obie get a little bit ahead of me.

We found the hut on the dirt road, all right. The door
was open, but no one was inside. There was a sound of
hammering from behind the house, so we went around
to the back. There was a man pounding away at a chicken
coop. I knew right away that it was Pa. He wasn't so
tall or so handsome-looking as I remembered, but he
was so wonderfully real.

"D'you want something, boys?" he asked, looking at
us in a queer, kind of wondering way. I didn't know
that I remembered his voice, but as soon as I heard it,
I did.

How do you tell somebody you haven't seen for five
years that you're his sons? We just stared at him, and he
stared back at us. Then Obie said it.

"Pa, it's us, Obie and Amos."

Pa put down his hammer and looked at us the way a
starving man might look at food. "I knew it," he said
softly, almost to himself. "My own boys, Amos and Obie.
Five hundred miles, though. How'd you ever come?
Five hundred miles!"

He hugged us tight, and I knew right then that all

the being on our own, and walking in the dark, and being scared of our own footsteps was over. We'd made it to our new home.

Late that night Obie and I were lying on a blanket in the corner of the room. From where I lay I could see Pa, sitting at the table, writing a letter in the flickering candlelight. The letter was for the Preacher. Some evening, maybe in September, he would again visit our little cabin and read the letter to Mama and Sally.

My mind went back across the weeks and the miles to his first visit and the first letter. It had been May, a warm Sunday evening. It seemed so long ago. I was trying to remember something, trying to get hold of some kind of pattern, and I couldn't quite do it.

"Obie," I whispered, "remember when the Preacher came the first time and you were just talking to Mama?"

There was no answer.

"Remember, you were telling her about Abraham, how he got called and he went out, and he didn't know where?"

But Obie was sound asleep.